FOUR CORNERS

K. A. Strickland

***

KAS Publishing

and

Mythical Legends Publishing

Four Corners is a work of fiction. The characters, incidents, and dialogs are products of the author's imagination and are not to be construed as real. Any resemblance to actual events or persons, living or dead, is entirely coincidental.

A KAS/Mythical Legends Publishing Mass Market Paperback

Copyright © 2013 by Kenneth A Strickland
Published by KAS and Mythical Legends, 2013
Publisher@mythicallegends.com
http://mythicallegends.com

ISBN-10: 0962783579
ISBN-13: 978-0-9627835-7-9

Printed in the United States of America

9 8 7 6 5 4 3 2 1

DEDICATION

This book is dedicated to all the great dreamers
     Who taught me how to dream . . .
   That includes my dad (who said it was okay to be who I was),
   Every book I've ever read, every movie I've ever seen,
     . . . And every dream that I ever had the chance to remember . . .

ACKNOWLEDGMENTS

To all those who are on this journey with me . . .

1. DRIVING INTO TOWN

It was a hot sticky southern afternoon.

Joyce Madisen, a pretty blonde, drove her '68 Mustang with the windows rolled up, and the air conditioner high. Her favorite Rod Stewart tape played and she sang along with the raspy voice; "if you want my body and you think I'm sexy, come on baby tell me so . . ."

She glanced at her gauges and saw the needle was almost on 'E'.

"Oh, shit. . . ." she said with no small disgust, "you would do this to me." She looked around and saw a sign coming up. Four corners, six miles. Joyce rolled her eyes heavenward and said, "Thank you! Thank you!" She eased back on the speed and prayed her fuel would hold out long enough to get her to the town she hoped would be her salvation.

Night was falling.

Joyce smiled as she came into town and pulled into the first gas station she came to. It had a cashier's cage with a small snack shop attached.   There was a youngish, burly man wearing overalls, dark glasses and a plaid shirt with a not too friendly look to him.

She pulled up to the pumps. "Evenin', ma'am, what can I do for you?" He was about six foot even, and he was appraising her coldly from behind the dark glasses....dark glasses at sunset?

"Fill me up, regular." Joyce said. "Do you have a restroom?"

He pointed. "Right around the corner, and they're clean. I know city folks are worried about things like that."

Joyce gave a nervous smile. "Thanks. That's nice to know." She got out of the car and walked backward a few steps staring at the man as he filled her car. He was big, with a bulge around his middle.

Joyce did her business then went back to her car. The big man watched her from shaded eyes, trying not to make contact with her. "That'll be twenty-two fifty."

"You take plastic?"

"Yeah,"

She handed her card to him and he went to the small cashier's cage, made out the charge receipt, then came back and handed it to her to sign. As he did so, Joyce watched as the bulge under his clothes seemed to give a slight move, as if the bulge was trying to break loose from the restraint. She looked twice, and was sure the second time. Some thing was under his clothes.

The man took the signed receipt and gave her the customer copy.

"I guess you eat well." Joyce said. "Is there a place around here I can get a meal and some sleep?"

"Right across the street at the hotel; funny y'all didn't see it when you drove up." The big man said. "Sign's all lit up."

"I guess when you're not thinking, you don't see things."

"Reckon you don't." He watched as Joyce got in her car and drove over to the parking lot of the hotel and coffee shop. At the sight of the coffee shop, Joyce remembered how hungry she was. She parked, and then went inside.

Joyce wondered if she'd made the biggest mistake of her life. There was an empty stool at the counter that she took. She placed her purse at her feet, and smiled at the waitress who wore dark glasses like the big man at the gas station. Joyce smiled, but the woman didn't smile back.

Were all the people in this town unfriendly?

"What's on the menu?" Joyce asked, trying to break the ice.

"Fish is good, fresh caught this morning. We got the best fried chicken in these parts, and there's still some soup left, that's corn chowder, made with fresh corn."

"Of course fresh corn," Joyce smiled.

"You from New York? You sound like it." The waitress asked,

"Uhm, yeah, Manhattan; on my way back home from vacation," replied Joyce.

"I hope you had a good time."

"I did." She looked over the menu for a moment, then said; "I'll have the fried chicken. I really shouldn't, but I have taste for it tonight."

"You'll love it." The waitress took the menu and placed the order with the cook, who also wore dark glasses.

Joyce looked around as careful as possible.

Everyone wore dark glasses.

This made no sense. Joyce had the feeling that if she asked, she'd get a brush off. As she looked a little closer, doing her best not to look like she was looking, she saw the same peculiar bulge under the clothes. There was a family in a booth in the corner to her right. Even the children and she knew that only when the little boy got up and ran around the restaurant until his father, who had the same bulge as everyone else, got up and grabbed him by the arm and sat him down.

Joyce contained her curiosity as tight as she could. She hoped she could fall asleep tonight now that she had a major bone to chew.

The waitress set her food in front of Joyce who thanked her.

Suddenly, the waitress did a quick frantic wave to someone behind Joyce who turned to see what looked like a young man drop to the ground. Outside of the restaurant, the young man Joyce thought she saw scurried away in a crawling motion, turned the corner of the building, then got up and ran across the street to the gas station.

"That fool's gonna try and come in here naked!" The waitress said. "He bet me he'd do it too!" She turned away from Joyce and said to the kitchen; "Get that fool Purdy's lunch! I don't know what he thinks he's gonna do trying to come in here like that! Marshall, you run over to where he is and give him this, and tell him if he does that again, we're gonna have an extra piece o' sausage for breakfast! You hear me?"

Joyce laughed as she dug into her food, and she kept an eye on Marshall who picked up two sacks with the food and left. She tried to follow him as he left the store, but didn't turn her head as he left her sight. Why the excitement?

Joyce had the feeling something was up, and there was some kind of cover up that was going on. It was dark, and even so, Marshall wore a pair of dark sunglasses. It had occurred to Joyce that he never looked in her direction.

What if her frantic little wave wasn't about a man's nudity?

As she ate, that funny little feeling she always got when something was going on gnawed at her.

"She just started eating," Marshall said as he approached the sheriff, Jim Mosley. "Marcy sent me out to get Purdy his lunch. He was gonna try to get in there naked like he said he would, and Marcy chased him off before he could get in on account of that woman. You know she's sweet on Purdy, but she didn't want that woman seeing him."

"It wasn't for him being butt naked, and you know that, Marshall." Mosley said. "I saw her license plate. She's from New York."

Marshall looked at the coffee shop. "I hope this is just a stopover for her. Hate to see anything happen to her."

"Me, too," Mosley said. "If she leaves in the morning, fine. I don't even want to think about what could happen." He slapped Marshall on the back. "Go get Purdy his lunch. You know he works the late shift."

"Yeah," Marshall walked down about a quarter mile to a dirt road, then another quarter until the main road disappeared behind the trees that hid the building Purdy worked at from view. He walked up to the electrified gate pulling out a plastic identification card, sliding it in to the box's slot that hung next to the electronic lock. Two lights flashed, and he slid his right hand onto a panel with the outline of a hand on it. The gate slid open enough to allow Marshall in, and then closed. He made his way up to the door, stood in front of the camera, waited for the buzz, and then went inside.

"Hey Marshall,"

"Hey Dave,"

"Did Purdy order out?" Dave Marcus asked as he spotted the two sacks in Marshall's hands.

"Naw, but I brought you a ham sandwich, milk and piece of pie." He handed the sack to Dave who happily opened it.

"Thanks for the pie. Jenny's been on me to lose some weight, and if she finds out I've some of Marcy's pie, she'll kill me." Dave pulled out the food and placed it on the small table in front of him. "Y'know, this is one the things that drive me crazy with Purdy, his going to get some food and him not asking if I want anything."

"Didn't Jenny make you a lunch?"

"Yeah, but y'know how it is; Low fat, low calories and low taste," Dave said. "I just wish she'd let me eat normal. I'd be happier."

"I'll bet." Marshall said. "Look, we got a stranger in town, and she's at the coffee shop. I think she planning' to stay overnight, and then go on in the morning. At least I hope so."

"I hope so too." Dave said "This is the only place I can let all four arms hang out with no problems."

"Well, I envy you. You can be comfortable; I got to be bound up like a turkey at Thanksgiving."

"Why do you think I took this job?"

"Cause your daddy got it for you."

Dave shrugged. "You've got me there." Both men laughed.

"Anyway, I'd better get back. When Purdy gets back, give him his lunch."

"Right, see you later."

"See you later." Marshall left, whistling. Dave turned back to his lunch when he heard the door to his right open. In came Purdue Jackson "Purdy" McClain. He was trying to retie his necktie, which he hated, but it was company policy that employees wear them. He finally made a sloppy knot as Dave looked at him in disgust.

"You just had to try that stunt, didn't you?" Dave said as the younger man went to the desk, saw the other sack and picked it up.

"I told her I would try it." Purdy was a dirty blond haired young man of twenty-three, who lived most of his life in Four Corners. Five foot eight, on the thin side, he had a crooked smile that complemented his bright hazel eyes. " 'sides, the bet's still on."

"Well, I'm glad that stranger didn't see you," said Dave as he lifted his carton of milk. "The last thing we need is some stranger seeing you trying to win some silly bet!"

"She didn't see me." Purdy said as he bit into his sandwich. "Since she didn't see me, ain't no harm done."

Dave shook his head in disgust. "Why do you have to learn everything the hard way?"

"That ain't fair. . ." Purdy started.

"I ain't talking about fair!" Dave exploded. "I'm talking about the lives of everyone in this town! Don't you get it? We could lose everything if we're found out." He picked up his food and walked away. "You're too damn selfish to be eatin' with."

"Dave, aw, come on!" Purdy said as the older man went to the lunchroom. He slumped on his stool.

Damn him for being right.

2. TRUCKING GONE WRONG

Cody Macabee woke up. He closed his eyes again trying to make the room stop swimming.

It didn't work.

He also couldn't move. He lifted his head and saw he'd been restrained at all four wrists.

At least he still had all four arms. His double pupil eyes searched around the room.

A hospital….

He was in a hospital.

Cody figured he'd been searched, samples taken, and then strapped down.

Wonderful….

He laid his head back, took a deep breath. He had to assume that everything had been taken, and his truck. . .

He gave a heavy, depressed sigh.

It all came back in a rush. Driving down the interstate, he'd hit a patch of ice, the big rig jackknifing uncontrolled, with him fighting it, trying to get stopped, when the truck rolled. He hit his head against something, and was out.

Damn.

Damn again.

This was the last thing he or anyone else from Four Corners needed.

He was grateful for one thing; the liquid he was hauling wasn't flammable. But did any of it leak? They built those tanks to be as bulletproof as possible, but that didn't mean a spill couldn't happen.

Cody shuddered with the fear that what he hauled might get into the water supply. It was extremely toxic, and would burn flesh even if were diluted. He had to call home.

Cody pulled on the straps with all four arms. No good, the anchors had to be welded to the bed, and the straps were new, and he didn't have the leverage. He stopped struggling.

Voices were coming down the hall toward him.

The door opened, and the bright light forced him to close his eyes and turn his head.

"Well, I guess you're awake." A man's voice said.

"Do you mind?" Cody said. "I can't see you."

"I guess with those double pupil eyes, you would be sensitive to bright light." The man said.

"Very good," Cody said. "You now have two dollars, would you like to try for four?"

"There's no need to be sarcastic. . ." the man said.

"Being tied down does nothing for my mood," returned Cody. "Why am I tied down?"

"Well, son, we're not too sure about you." Another man said as the room lights came on. "Here you are driving a truck. . ."

"Not against the law," said Cody.

". . . You've got four arms. . ." the second man continued.

"Still not against the law,"

"We tested the stuff you were hauling'. That stuff was so toxic it'll burn on contact. Where were you hauling it?" The second man asked.

Cody turned to the voice and a craggy face with balding head came into focus. The man the questioning voice belonged to had pale gray eyes and disappearing brown hair that was graying at the temples. "Did it spill?"

"You know that stuff is toxic?" baldy asked.

"Why do you think my company put a disposal facility twenty miles away from the plant? It was a safety measure." Cody said his eyes closing. "Did any of it spill?"

The four people that entered the room looked at each other.

"I'm dealing with assholes here. DID IT SPILL? Do I have to paint a sign for you?" Cody was exasperated. "Lord, wood floats."

"What do you know about it?" asked baldy.

Cody lifted his head and banged it against his pillow. "DID THAT SHIT SPILL?! THAT IS MORE IMPORTANT THAN ANYTHING ELSE YOU WANT TO ASK ASSHOLE!! DID IT SPILL?!?"

The room went silent for a long time. The bald man said; "Look, you have to understand we are curious. . ."

Cody looked as if he was going to sink through the bed. "Lord, they must be government people, that's the only reason why I can't get the answer I need. . .   Give   me   strength, please."

"It didn't spill."

"Thank you. Finally...!" Cody said his body relaxing. "Can we have some names to go with these faces? I figure you've already gone through my wallet."

The bald man looked at his companions, and their looks all said the same thing: Cody would say nothing until he knew who he was talking to, and very little then.

The craggy bald man spoke first. "My name is Taylor, Dane Taylor, Department of Unusual Phenomena. When your accident was reported, and you were found unconscious, I was called in."

There's a Department of Unusual Phenomena?" Cody was incredulous.

"Don't laugh. What with aliens with star bases, and who knows what, we figure it's best to be prepared." Taylor said.

"That explains why I'm strapped down," reasoned Cody. "I guess I would fall under your jurisdiction. I really need this like a hole in the head." He thought a moment, and then asked, "Did anyone other than you and the witnesses see me?"

"The trucker who found you did. Your shirt had been ripped, and he quite clearly saw your other arms." Taylor told him. He glanced at the others in the room. All could see the wheels turning in his head.

"I take my one phone call is out of the question?" Cody asked.

"No, it isn't. But we would like to ask you some questions." Taylor said.

Cody sighed. "Look, I'm a mutant. I was born this way."

The first man spoke up. "Uhm, my name is Doctor Thurston Harris." He held out his hand then caught himself when he realized Cody couldn't take it in return. "Do you know what caused your mutation?"

"No, I don't." Cody said. "I'm not a scientist." Cody knew he was lying, but it was in self-defense. In truth, he held two degrees in chemical engineering, and one in biological engineering. He most likely knew more than this whole team of experts now in his room.

"You know, Cody, lying is not very good." Dane Taylor said. "While you were unconscious, I looked you up; Three degrees, with two in chemical engineering, one in bioengineering. Why would a truck driver need that kind of education?"

Cody groaned on the inside. He was hoping they hadn't looked him up while he was out. He felt the stares burn into him. "Mind if I plead the fifth for now? I really would like a lawyer present for any questioning."

"Until we know different, you're still a citizen of the U.S." Taylor said. "One way or the other, we will find out."

"Joy beyond words," Cody spoke. "May I make my call?"

"Why not...?" Taylor said. He turned to Harris. "Un-strap him . . ."

"You think that's wise?" Harris was nervous about Cody as it was, he didn't want to untie him at all.

"A man with three degrees is not stupid. Am I right, Cody?" Taylor said.

"I don't care to be shot while making a daring escape. Too fifties and I would like to stretch. I'm staying put," said Cody.

Harris was not happy. "Are you sure about this?"

"If it makes you feel any better, Harris, I don't trust you either. You look real eager to slice me up."

"Now wait a minute!" Harris started.

"Un-strap him..!" Taylor said firmly. "We've got the trank guns ready."

Doctor Harris pulled set of keys out of his pocket, chose one, and then unlocked the straps. Cody got up slowly as Harris quickly backed away. Stopping in mid-rise to allow his head to clear, Cody took several deep breaths, his lungs filling to their limit, and then exhaling. He sat up, braced himself with his two lower arms while rubbing his head and neck with the upper pair.

A woman approached him. "You have double pupils in your eyes."

"You have single pupils in yours." replied Cody, removing the hospital robe to examine his sore left side. "Oh, man!" He touched it gingerly, "Barbecued. . ." He looked at Harris. "Where are my clothes?"

"I told you he was going to try to leave!" Harris said moving closer to the door.

"I've got more to fear from you than you have of me. I'd like to walk down the hall like a decent person. Do you mind you panicky jackass?" Cody said. He slid off the bed and went to the closet. "Thank you, Lord, my bag is here!"

Cody was completely indifferent to his nudity. His every move was economical as he dressed from the undamaged clothes in the tough canvas covered Kevlar bag. Out came the pants (he never did like underwear), then a four-armed shirt.

"Your other shirt wasn't four armed. . ." the woman said.

"How many times in the movies or television do you see an actor were clothes to disguise that he's only playing handicapped? In my case, it's the reverse."

"Aren't you afraid of peoples' reactions?" She asked.

"What's your name?"

"Ah, Doctor Theresa St. Thomas." She said, a bit nervous.

"Well, Doctor St. Thomas, I have been seen, and there's no way for me to deny what I am, not that I would. I'd prefer that no one knew, but I have no doubt that I have been seen by more people than you can keep quiet." He zipped shut the bag, then finished dressing. "Damn." He turned to Taylor. "I take it we leave now?"

"What do you mean?" asked Taylor.

"Don't play stupid. You are waiting for me to be released, aren't you?" Cody asked.

"Well, yes." replied Taylor.

"Let's get on with it. I need to make my call." Cody reached into a side pocket of the bag and pulled out a pair of dark glasses and put them on. He opened the door and was grateful for the glasses. Camera flashes went off in his face and there was a woman with her cameraman who stuck her microphone in his face and said; "Katherine McKinley, CNN. Who are you, are you an alien, and are you part of a vanguard of some invasion fleet?"

"Tell me, are you really a journalist, or do you always go around asking silly questions?" Cody asked with disgust.

"Well, let's face it, a four armed man in a trailer truck accident? That is a story, you know." McKinley said. "Look, just a few questions, okay?"

"You know something?" Cody said, "People like you are like alcoholics, one question's too many, and a thousand don't begin to satisfy you."

"Look, I'm just the first, and there a lot more outside." She said as she and her cameraman kept pace with Cody. "You don't realize you can give me an exclusive and get out the back way."

"I can still get out the back way without talking to you." said Cody.

"Really…?" McKinley told him. "I know the guy walking with you is from the DUP. Dane Taylor is one of the best they've got, and if he's here, there's a story. You're it."

A heavy silence hung over the hall as Cody thought about it. She would have to be right. If there had to be speculation, at the very least there could be something behind it. He didn't have to tell everything. He spotted a clock on the wall. Four a.m., and already he hated himself for what he had to do to get out of there.

"Let me make a couple of calls." Cody said. "That hand basket to hell is getting hotter by the minute."

"Where are you placing the call?" McKinley asked as Cody fished for his wallet out of his bag.

Cody grinned wickedly and said: "Darlin', that's why you do research."

The first went to his home to inform his father he was all right.

"Pop?"

"Cody, you all right, Boy?" Bodine Macabee asked anxiously as he silently gave thanks for his son being alive. "When we heard about the crash, we feared the worst."

"Well, I'll tell you right now, pop, I ain't doing too well right now. You hear of a Department of Unusual Phenomena?"

"Oh, dear Lord..! They got you boy?" Bodine asked.

"I never heard of them." Cody said.

"Boy they were set up after all the stuff happened in California, They investigate things like you and me and this town. I'll get Billy over to their headquarters in Atlanta. I know you were seen, so all I can tell you is say as little as possible, you gonna call the company?"

"Yeah,"

"You do that. I'll notify the mayor and Gertie. She'll tell the rest of the town; any news people there?"

Cody looked at McKinley, a frown forming on his face. "Unfortunately, yes."

Bodine went silent for a moment. "All I can say, boy, is just telling them as much truth as you think you can get away with. Lord knows they're gonna blow it out of proportion any way. . ."

"Tell me about it, pop. I'm callin' the company now." Cody said. "Pray for us, pop."

"Everybody started already, boy." Bodine said as he hung up.

The second call.

"Dave?"

"Cody? Thank God you're alive!" Dave Marcus said. He was sitting at a computer console the displayed a map showing where Cody and the big rig were. The light flashed alternate green/red. . . Signaling an accident, but the rig was intact.

"I don't know how you're gonna feel after I tell just how deep we're in it. I haven't seen the truck yet, but I've been told by the locals that it's still intact. If it is, I'll drive to the disposal site and they'll take it from there."

"Right; well, my board says the same thing. The sensors say that nothing leaked, although someone took a sample amount from the tank, probably for analysis. All I can say is be careful, man. That stuff hasn't been neutralized yet, and I don't even want to think of what happens if we get into a disaster situation." Dave said. "If it were up to me, I'd have you sit tight until we got a team to you." He paused and thought about it for a moment. "I tell you what, sit tight, and don't let anyone near that truck. I'll have a team get to you within four hours to take over from you. They'll have a new tractor to pull it and haul your tractor back to the shop for any needed work. See if you can get a hotel room and call from there. You might want to get some sleep, this gonna be a long one, Cody."

"I know. Tell everyone I'm sorry." Cody said.

"Nobody's gonna blame you. It wasn't your fault." Dave said.

"Yeah, right," Cody said.

The two men let it hang in the air. Thirty years they kept the secret of Four Corners and its people. When he walked out the room he made the calls in, it would be all over.

Cody didn't like himself very much now. "Bye, Dave."

"Good luck, we're praying for you." Dave said.

It took Cody a while to put the phone back since he'd made his calls and there wasn't anything he could do until the relief team got here. Now he had to deal with the reporter, DUP man, and try to find a place to sleep.

He wished he hadn't forgotten the hose for his fan.

3. SHE'S LEAVING TOWN

Joyce didn't sleep at all that night. She kept turning over in her mind the people of this town acted odd.

Scratch that, odd wasn't strong enough.

Bizarre was more like it.

Why the dark glasses at night? Was there something wrong about their eyes?

Those bulges in the middle of even the thinnest person she'd seen?

That guy, Purdy; Why did he drop so fast when Marcy, the waitress waved at him?

She rolled the questions in her mind for the longest time, and realized she wasn't going to get any sleep until she got to the bottom of this.

Joyce dressed quickly and then sat in the darkened motel room, taking deep breaths, and then breathing normally. She let her memories and observations of the evening flow through her mind, everything taking place before her inner eye in slow motion.

The waitress's middle seemed to shift unnaturally.

So did the man at the gas station.

So did apparently everyone else's.

The odd shape of the thin man's torso, the one who sat on the stool a few seats away from her...

It didn't taper like it should have, just like everyone else.

Something was wrong with their bodies. What?

The bulge at his stomach wasn't like any she'd seen.

Then it hit her.

The bulge shifted. As if it was trying to get comfortable.

No.

Impossible....

What would make that so?

Trying to hide something, of course....

An animal...?

No, a furry head would have popped up, she was sure of that.

Joyce got up from her bed and went to her window, glad that it faced the gas station. She saw the man who had filled her car up get into his truck. Perfect, she would follow him. She ran out of her room, got in her car, prayed she wasn't getting in over her head as she started the car, and then drove off.

She caught up with the truck in a couple of miles, and then dropped behind it about hundred yards. It was dark, but as long as she kept the truck's taillights in her sight, she wouldn't lose him.

The truck went on for about thirty minutes, until it came to a two-lane blacktop. Joyce allowed him one minute's distance, then drove on, knowing she could catch him soon enough.

She was right. She caught him just as he was turning onto a dirt road that led up to a house with a barn and a few smaller buildings.

Joyce turned off her lights and parked. She reached into her glove compartment and pulled out an extra heavy-duty flashlight, a camera loaded with high-speed film along with a pair of heavy leather gloves. She got out of the Mustang and stepped carefully toward the house. The man in the truck had gotten out as she was getting ready to do so, stretched, and pulled off his shirt. Joyce didn't know why, but something told her to shoot pictures as he removed his shirt.

To her credit, Joyce didn't scream when she saw his two lower arms unfurl from his body, stretch, do a few wide arcs in the air, then drop to his side. Joyce took several photos as she watched him, and as he walked the porch light and stretched again, she got off several shots of him in full extension. Joyce decided not to push her luck and got back to her car.

Joyce ran as hard as she could, opened the car door, sat in the seat and slid the ignition key in. A figure popped up in her rear view mirror, grabbed her, pressed a cloth to her face, and held it there forcing her to breathe it in. She passed out on the front seat of her Mustang.

Four other figures ran to the car. Sheriff Jim Mosley directed the deputies to put the car on the trailer behind the house, and put Joyce in it. Mosley took her purse and wallet in rubber-gloved hands, examined the contents, then said; "Make sure she gets back home to New York City. Shouldn't be down here in this part of Georgia any way. . ."

Joyce Madisen woke up in her apartment in New York, in her pajamas. Looking around, she stared at the familiar surroundings as if seeing them for the first time. She touched her pajamas, feeling the material, and then looked around again.

Impossible....

She searched her memory, trying to remember what happened to her. She tried to stand up, collapsing back on the bed. A wave of nausea hit her, and she staggered/crawled into her bathroom to throw up. When she was finished, she gulped air until her head stopped throbbing.

Mike Conners, the Mayor of Four Corners walked into Jim Mosley's office. Mosley looked up from his newspaper as his brother in law came in. "Anything wrong, Mike..?"

"That woman who drove into town last night; what happened to her?" Conners asked. "I was not told how she followed Hank all the way to his house, and then took pictures!"

"Mike, there wasn't much you could have done about it." Mosley said, putting his paper down. "Besides, we got the film, and when she takes the roll we replaced it with in for developing and the pictures come out blank, she'll think she dreamed the whole thing. Relax!"

Conners took out a handkerchief and mopped his brow. He was half black since most of the town came to realize they couldn't very well marry outside of the city limits. All the people in the county who'd been affected by the mutagenic in their food and water quickly came to ignore the differences in race. It had become a moot point. The old bloodlines between ex-slave and master had been mixing for more than twenty years now. That Mosley, son of a Klu-Klux-Klan member had no problems with his sister marrying Mike spoke volumes about the entire situation in Four Corners.

"All I can say is I just want that woman to wake up thinking she had a weird dream." Conners told him. "The press card you found in her purse does not make me happy."

"Think I'm happy about it?" Mosley said. "There ain't one person in the entire town who ain't worried about it. Thing is, we can't go off half cocked because she showed up." He cleared his throat. "Sorry about that. Look, I'm not gonna worry about it until something happens. I advise you to do the same. You and Jenny gonna be over for Sunday supper?"

"Oh, yeah, you know how I love Callie's cooking. She is making her peach cobbler?" Conners asked as he stood up.

"She's always makes that even after the peaches are not in season, and she canned a few bushels, you know that. You are bringing some of your ice cream?" Mosley asked.

"Course I am, now that I know we got the cobbler." Conners said as he left.

"Callie figured you would." Mosley went back to his paper.

In New York, Joyce made her way to a one-hour photo developer shop near her house to get the roll of film she remembered taking developed. It had occurred to her she'd taken the pictures as she went through her bags. She had other rolls of film from her vacation she would have done at the same time, but the one she remembered was in her camera was the one that was most important. She dropped the film off, and then went to work.

As she entered the newsroom of station WNYC and its NEWSCAMERA SIX logo, she heard the voice of Nick Mancuso greet her with; "Well, look who graces us with her presence! Our shining star comes back to the peons who love you."

Joyce gave him a sour look.

"Don't tell me your vacation didn't work, not after that call you gave me the night before last asking me for another day off so you could recover from your drive. . ." Nick said.

"Wait, wait, wait, and wait a minute . . . what phone call?" Joyce asked.

"Come on! Your call where your speech was all slurred, and you sounded really wasted. . . "Nick started.

"Hold it . . . I sounded wasted?" Joyce said. "You know I don't even drink!"

"Well, I got news for you." Nick told her. "When you called my place up, you sounded like you partied all the way in. Heh! I don't even know how you got past the toll booths!" He handed her a sheaf of papers. "Look, now that you're back, can we get some work out of you? The mayor's giving a press conference at noon today. I figured we'd start you on something light. . ."

Joyce hadn't heard him. "You're saying I called you drunk, asking for another day off to recover?"

"Yeah . . ."

"About what time did I call you?" Joyce asked.

Nick thought about it. "It's on my telephone's call log. I'd have to look it up. Why do you ask?"

A slow look of fear crossed her face. "Nick, I never called you. . ."

"Joyce, this is me you're talking to," Nick said. "I know your voice."

"Nick, I'm telling you, something happened to me, and I don't know what." Joyce said, an edge of fear creeping into her voice. "Let's go to your office, please?"

"Nick, this is going to sound real stupid." She said as they went into his office, Nick closing the door behind him. "Look, you know I don't drink." She sat down; put her hands in her face.

"You okay, Madisen?" Nick asked. "Can I get you anything?"

Joyce took her face away from her hands. "How long have we known each other?"

"Six years." Nick answered.

"Have you ever known me to go off on wild flights of fantasy about anything?" She asked.

"No. I've seen you go off about anything." He said.

"Exactly," Joyce said. She took a deep breath, then said, "I'm gonna tell you something, don't stop me until I'm finished."

She told him everything that she could remember, and what she saw when the gas station attendant took off his shirt, about how she took pictures, ran back to her car, then found herself with a face full of something that knocked her out.

Nick sat back, rubbed his chin, and said nothing.

Joyce was sure he didn't believe her after a story like that. "Look, just forget I said anything."

"I didn't say I didn't believe you." He said.

"I'm sorry." She said.

"What town did you say it was?" He asked.

"Four Corners, Georgia." Joyce said. "You believe me?"

"Look, we've got aliens with a star base in Northern California, why shouldn't you have seen a guy with four arms in a small town in Georgia?" Nick said. "Besides, there was a story not too long ago about a small town that fought back against a company that was dumping raw sewage in a river that ran past there. They took them to court and won, big. The company would've have shut down, but the town turned around and showed them how they could clean up the act and have more efficient production while they were at it. It seems they've been very good at how to have clean and profitable industry. Matter of fact it's main thing in that town . . . how to make industry more environmentally friendly and profitable at the same time."

"But you think they may have more to them than that?" asked Joyce.

"I've no doubt of it. What I want you to do is research that town. I want our facts straight on this." Nick said. "I grew up in a town not too far from there. Sometime in the fifties, and this was never confirmed, it was said something like thalidomide babies were being born there, only no one could find them."

"You think maybe those babies were hidden?"

"I'd say it's real possible. A lot of the local water got so bad, you couldn't drink it. There were several factories around there that didn't really bother cleaning up their sludge and crap before dumping in the water supply. People were getting sick, and moms who were having babies didn't show those kids off from what I heard. Mind you, this is all speculation.

But, a couple of times, people would go over there and find that the town had changed. It had gotten all closed off to outsiders. Oh, they were as friendly as they needed to be, but not if you wanted to move there. I think what happened to you may be a part of whatever's going on."

"You want me to find out?" Joyce asked.

"It might be an interesting story." Nick said. "Tell you what; you do the research from outside. We'll both look at it, and we may find something that'll shed some light on the subject."

"Right; What if I don't find anything?" Joyce asked.

"Get real. Anybody interested enough to follow you to put you to sleep, must be hiding something." Nick told her. "Get to it. I wanna know why you were knocked out."

Joyce got her things and said, "So do I." and then left.

4. RUNAWAY TRAINS

1919-1920

"Well, Mister Welles, what do you think?" Henry McCarran asked as he waved his out spread arms at the land before them. There was a beautiful river before them, gorgeous, fertile land with trees and brush. Birds were singing, and the wildflowers were in full bloom.

"Too beautiful for a factory, more like a site for a home." Stanley Welles said as he looked over the land. "You sure about the town council..?"

"In my pocket, huh..?" McCarran said, smiling. "They're desperate for work so people won't desert the town. We'll employ, oh, about two hundred people in our furniture factory. We'll have showrooms, and the railroad has promised to make this town a stop, so we can ship our products. It can't miss!"

"You know, Hank, I had my doubts, but, now that I see it, it has possibilities." Welles told his partner. "Still, we should be careful. Too fast, and we can blow the whole deal. I don't like the idea of building a two million dollar factory, and having it does a belly flop into red ink."

"Stan, you've always been a worrier." McCarran said, taking off his hat, running his fingers in his hair, and then putting the hat back on. "But then again, you have kept me from making big mistakes in the past, and I appreciate it. Don't worry like you normally do. This will work." The two men walked back to their car and drove off.

One year later, the workers at the new Welles-McCarran furniture factory cheered as the first piece, a chest of drawers, came off the line.

The Welles-McCarran factory was joined by the Hanover-Dury-McTeague factory. They manufactured cloth.

Bailey Manufacturing Company joined them later that same year. They made pulp and paper products.

All three were successful.

All three dumped much of their sewage into the river.

The sewage began its slow absorption into the ecosystem, and into the bodies of the people who used the water for irrigating their farms for food, their cooking and drinking.

But the changes took a long, long time.

Through the depression, through the Second World War, the factories continued their output.

The people continued to use the more and more tainted water.

Finally it happened.

1947

Henry and Abigail Lemon struggled through the difficult birth.

The midwife finally got the baby out and nearly dropped it when she saw what she had.

Henry looked at his son and withdrew in horror. He ran outside after grabbing the shotgun he kept over his mantle, put it in his mouth and pulled the trigger.

Abigail demanded to see her child. She screamed, turned her head and cried inconsolably.

The child was the first of the new, mutant children.

Abigail would have done as her husband did, but a doctor named Sam Murdock, asked to have the child. "Let me see what happened to your baby, Abigail."

"That's not my baby," she replied, "my baby died."

Murdock understood, and took the boy from her. He didn't kill the baby boy, but took it home and examined the child.

Murdock did all that he could in 1947 to understand what happened to the child during gestation. He saw the double pupil eyes, the four arms, and when he listened to the heart, he found two beating hearts beneath the chest.

Five more were born that year. Three were killed outright by distraught parents, two, Sam Murdock saved. He raised the three as his own, and when they asked about their parents, they were told they had died. Period . . .

Over the next few years, the parents of the town found themselves giving birth to the mutant children. Most had four arms and double pupil eyes, some found themselves with three arms, or four hands, or any number of limbs, or none at all.

Murdock and the other doctors watched as the town started to lose grip on its sanity. They called a town meeting to try and calm everyone down. This was in 1954.

Murdock was joined by Doctors Raymond and Williams who sat at a table on the stage of the auditorium at Welles high school.

Out in the audience were the townspeople along with their children, many who were mutants.

Murdock gaveled the meeting to order. He allowed the silence to settle on the meeting and hoped they would listen to him and his colleagues. "I realize that the births in the last few years have been difficult. . ."

"Difficult?" Lonny Vincent said, "We're birthin' monsters!"

"Not monsters, mutants." Raymond said.

"What are you talking about?" Lonny asked angrily. "My wife stopped me from doing the right thing when that freak was born! I have a right to see to it I have a normal child!"

"Lonny," Williams said softly, "I got one too, but that don't mean I'm gonna kill it. There is a reason why this is happening, and we all want to know what it is. I am as horrified about this as any of you. But there is something inside our bodies that is making this happen."

"What's that got to do with anything?" Lonny said, furious, "you ain't saying it's my fault?"

"We're not saying it's anybody's fault, Lonny." Raymond said.

"Lonny, sit down and shut up, and let these men finish!" Mayor Robert Taylor said. "It's high time we started trying figure out what's going on here, and if there's any way to change what's happened. That does not gonna happen if you don't sit down. We need facts, not fear!"

Lonny said, "I'm scared, bless it all!" He broke down, dropping to his seat, resting his head on the seat in front of his, and cried. The crowd understood what he was feeling, but the mayor was right, they needed to think, not panic.

"I think we all understand what Lonny's feeling right now. I know I do." Williams said "When I saw my little girl at birth, I hung my head and cried. I thought the wrath of the Lord was on me."

"I think we all know now, that if this is happening to just about everyone in town who've given birth, I think it's safe to say that whatever is causing this, is doing it to everyone in town. Am I right?" Murdock said.

There was murmuring throughout the crowd.

"Yeah but what do we do about it?" Jake Masters called from the back row. "These kids are gonna grow up, and we can't hide them forever. . ."

"No, we can't hide the children, but we will teach them how to hide what's different about them. But we will not panic, and most of all, we will not be ashamed of them.

Something frightening has happened. We can let it destroy us, or we can beat it."

"How we gonna beat it? We don't know what caused it!" Mercy Jean Hammond shouted. "How do we know we can beat this? If it's something in our bodies, we may never find out!"

"Mercy Jean, I believe we can find out what happened, but we are going to need your help." Raymond said firmly. "What we are going to have to do is learn, so we can change what's happened to us. I know it's too late for the children already here. They'll be all right if we work with each other. I want to get to the bottom of this like all of you."

"Mister Mayor?" Murdock said.

The mayor stood up and said; "We are gonna build a research center to study this. I have taken the liberty of buying two of the old Bailey buildings they no longer need and begun the conversion to research labs. Doctor Murdock?"

"This is what we're going to do. . ." Murdock said as youths went through the crowd handing out stapled sheets of four pages each. The plans were outlined in detail of the effort to get to the bottom of the mutations was outlined.

Grim faced, the assembled listened to the plan, not sure if they really wanted to, or if it were a pipe dream of finding some way to put an end to what some felt was a living nightmare.

It took them a year to put the buildings together and get the equipment to stock everything. The town was grim faced as the mutant births increased, and the town redoubled their efforts to get the labs established.

Within a year, all the residents in town had samples of every kind taken. They also started an intense school program that emphasized the sciences.

They taught their mutant children to hide their differences. Some in the town wanted to mutilate them by removing their second sets of limbs. That idea was shot down quick.

Still, many of the mutant children adjusted. Others did not.

Jake Kramer snapped at age ten, jumping off the tallest building in town, the town hall. This led to an intensified move by some to see to the mental health of the mutants. Some still abandoned their children, but they were taken in by others. Some would be parents sterilized themselves and left town. Some who had left found themselves coming back to Four Corners and finding out they were not alone in their horror at finding their children were mutated.

It wasn't easy, but the town did all that it could to make sure no one else found out what happened to them. Those who left never spoke of it to anyone.

1960

"You know, Doctor Murdock, I never realized how fascinating the field of genetics was until I heard you speak on the subject." Frank Morgan said as he and Sam Murdock walked down the hall at in the Sciences building at University of Georgia. "I still have a problem understanding how sewage dumped into the water may have a mutating effect."

Murdock smiled. He knew what the young doctor to be was saying, and was impressed by his grasp of the fundamentals of the course. "Well, it isn't the sewage in and of itself, but the chemical compounds in it, or what is formed when it is in the water for a long time. It isn't instant by any means, but a very gradual process that has to take a long time. Remember, that we're still just grasping the idea of how chemicals may affect the human body, no matter how long we've studied it, we still have much to learn."

"No doubt," Frank said.

'In any case, we're going to learn a lot more as we go along." Murdock said as they came to the top of the steps of the ornate building. "The field is wide open, of course, and we can go in any direction. My interest is in how chemicals affect the body if the compounds in action are unknown."

"I would think you'd go back to the source of the chemicals and analyze what went into them. If it's organic, say like something in water, but wasn't water soluble until it interacted with another chemical, then it might be able to affect an organic creature."

Murdock stopped in his tracks. Whether he knew it or not, Frank had hit on what had been eluding his team in Four Corners for some time. Of course, that had to be it. "Frank, do you think that an inorganic compound might mix with another, dissolve then combine with a third in the body?"

"I don't know, sir, you're the doctor." replied Frank.

"Well, you may have hit on something that I hadn't thought of yet." said Murdock.

"I'm sorry; I was just speaking out loud. . ." Frank said, not sure what his teacher was getting at.

"No, no, no. Water can wear away at something for a long time to wear it down. It can also take a longtime for something to reach the right proportions before it affects something." Murdock said as his eyes started to see something before him. His mind started to make some calculations as he said absentmindedly, "I want to thank you, Frank. You may have just solved me a very big puzzle." He ran down the step to his old Ford four door, got and drove away for the weekend.

"You're welcome, sir. . ." Frank said staring at the departing car.

"I tell you, Bill, this just might be the big piece of the puzzle we've been looking for." Sam Murdock said as he drove the Ford to the river.

"You think the compounds are in the river water?" Bill Reynolds had been dragged out of his office by his friend and colleague to the river's edge. In the trunk there were a dozen one-gallon glass jugs. "Explain to me about the jugs again."

"You're not that dense." Murdock said.

"No, I'm not that dense. But humor me," replied Reynolds as he drummed his fingers on the door of the car.

Murdock sighed. "Okay, fine have it your way. We're going to take the water we collect and analyze it, then take the samples of tissue and blood we've gathered over the years and see if any of the chemicals match."

"Why didn't we do this in the first place?" Bill asked.

"You really want to know?" asked Sam.

"Yeah,"

"We're not as smart as we think we are." Sam told him. "Besides, I don't see you coming up with any better ideas."

"Okay, I'm sorry."

"Thank you."

"You know, I think we might start trying to get some of the fluid from the currently pregnant moms and see if there are any traces in the fluid."

Sam shook his head. "You know, this has been pretty hard on everybody."

"Yeah, I know. The hardest part about it is that we didn't guess that it might be something we all had in common." Bill said as he stopped drumming his fingers on the car door. "The other day when I delivered Mazie Hawkins new boy, I could swear there was a slight greenish tint to her fluid. I got some on a towel, and I wondered why it was, so I put it in a sack and took it back to the lab. I haven't looked at it yet."

"You think her fluid had some of what we're looking for?" asked Sam as he parked the car.

Bill looked out the window, then at Sam. "I think so. That colored woman wept hard when she took that boy in her arms. Kept saying, "Lord, forgive me for my sins." over and over again. They gonna have to be brought into this. They just can't be left out any more."

"Most of them live right on the river, so they've been getting the water directly. . ." Sam said.

"You don't think the coloreds have been having the mutant babies before we started, do you?" asked Bill. He whistled. "That means if that's true, they've got mutant teenagers. . . ."

"That makes sense." Sam said. "Poor people, who really have nowhere else to go, get hit when things get rough first,"

"You want Jim with us when go to check out the other side of the tracks?" Bill asked.

Sam nodded. "We're gonna need another pair of hands when we get there." He parked the car, got out and took out two of the jugs then went to the river, held the jugs under the water, filled them, then got two more and did the same as Bill joined him.

Soon, all the jugs were filled and their caps twisted tight.

Sam stood up, looked at his colleague and said, "I want to go over to Mazie's house."

"You got your bag?" Bill asked, wiping his hands on his pants.

"Of course I do. What kind of doctor do you think I am?" Sam said indignantly.

Bill chuckled. "I just wanted to make sure."

"Uh huh," Sam said as they got in the car and drove off.

An hour later, Sam Murdock examined the baby boy who moved four perfectly shaped arms in circles. The twin heartbeats were listened to, and he and Bill agreed the child was in good health.

The baby's father, a big construction worker named Mordecai watched the two men intensely. "You must know somethin'."

Bill glanced at Sam, and then looked at him. "Why do you say that?"

"Two white doctors coming to this house right after the baby's born with four arms and two pupils in his eyes. I picked him up and listened to his heart, don't ask me why I did it, I just did. I heard two hearts beatin'. Now I may not know what y'all do, but I know somethin' in our bodies that done this. Done it to other babies, too. Somethin' is wrong here."

The two doctors looked at the big man. He'd put two and two together and didn't like the answer. "It's happened to us on our side of the tracks, too." Sam said quietly. "Have any of the other babies been killed, too?"

Mordecai shook his head. "Couldn't anybody kill the babies; I can't kill mine just cause of this. Our doctors can't tell us nothing about it. What's happenin' to us?"

Bill ran his finger through his hair. "We think it's got something to do with the water we use for everything."

"In the water?" asked Mordecai.

"In the water," Sam said.

Mazie brought glasses of lemonade and set them down on the table. "What's in the water?"

"We don't know yet." Bill told her. "We know there isn't any fish in the river now."

"Ain't been for twenty years," Mordecai said. "I got to go thirty miles just to fish."

"Whatever's in the water must have killed off the fish." Sam said, carefully choosing his words, "but by time it gets to us, it's not as bad."

"I don't know what you talking about. We gotta draw our water, like everybody else on this side of the tracks." Mazie said. "We ain't got running water."

Bill and Sam looked at each other. "Have you any other children?" Sam asked.

Mordecai and Mazie looked at each other. "We were hopin' this one would be right." Mazie said. "I love my children, but I want one who ain't like this."

"Anyone else have children like this?" Bill asked.

"Just about everyone around here, mister," Mordecai told them.

"You kept it secret?" Sam asked, "For how long?"

"I guess the first one came out about forty-seven, that right Mazie?" Mordecai said. "Just about every child since then is like that." He was pointing at his newborn son. "Tell me, mister doctor, why?"

"Why?" Were the hardest question he had to answer, and that one that was still a mystery to Doctor Sam Murdock; "Why?" taunted him, mocked him for the last ten years, and the answer was right in his face, and he almost couldn't see it. He looked at Mordecai and realized these people had been using the water directly for years, so their mutated children had been born much earlier. "Mordecai, I want you to think about what I'm going to ask you. To the best of your memory, when was the first four armed child born?"

Mordecai glanced over at his wife, who was picking up the child for the first time, he realized he had to do the same as so many parents on his side of town did, raise the child and teach it to hide his arms in plain sight. There was no lying to this man, now, he'd figured it out. He went over to the writing desk where his papers were. He did a quick search, then found an old, well kept three ring binder in a drawer, pulled it out and opened it. He then put on his glasses and read until he came to the first entry. "The first one of these children was born June six, nineteen hundred and forty five. The baby was found and taken in by Mama Dozier. She raised it, and went around to everybody who found out they had a four armed baby. . ."

Both doctors' mouths dropped.

". . . and saw to it that the babies survived by takin' 'em in." Mordecai finished and closed the book. "I guess you want to go find them?"

"Yes," Murdock said.

"They live in the old furniture factory," said Mordecai as he saw his wife breast feed the child for the first time. "Mostly because it's isolated now, since the owners deserted it. We do what we can, because we figured it wasn't happenin' to you white folks."

"It happened to us, only much slower." Reynolds said as he put the medical bag's contents back in. "I got one."

"Well, I guess us all in the same boat." Mordecai said as he put the book back.

"Why'd you keep the diary?" Murdock asked.

"Somebody had to." Mordecai answered. "Besides, I watch 'em some days, but I figure we gonna have to move 'em. Where, I don't know."

Bill looked at Sam, knowing what the black man meant. They were just as scared, and with the way most whites felt about blacks, it would be difficult at best, impossible at the worst to convince anyone that what happened to the blacks was important. "I don't think you have anything to fear, Mordecai, but it will be hard. Are they in school?"

"What schoolin' we can give 'em."

"Please, take us to them. I want to examine them. Please, it's important." Sam said, his eyes pleading with the skeptical man in front of him. "I think I can help."

"I can't just take you up there. Mama Dozier won't allow anyone to hurt them children. I tell her about you, but she may say no." Mordecai told him. "She runs that place with a firm hand, and don't care who you are if she thinks you're trouble. You gonna have to give me time."

Sam Murdock knew that was all he'd get for now. "Fine; But let her know what happening here is also happening with white people, please."

"Third time you've said please to me mister. You must be hurtin' bad." Mordecai said. "I tell you straight, I don't trust you. You make a big show of carin', but that don't mean nothin'. You could be just settin' us up for trouble."

"I'm not like that. . ." Murdock said.

"We'll see it in the bye and bye," said Mordecai. "We'll see."

5. WALKING ON BROKEN GLASS

Cody went to his big rig and inspected the damage. He went into his damaged cab and pulled out a large sample case that had been hardened to take abuse. It was black with hinged locks that fastened to the bottom edge of the case. A crowd gathered and watched him as he inspected the damage. Pulling out a set of safety goggles and gloves, he went around to every potential trouble area on the rig, visually checking the seal on the vent and double valve spigot. Going back to the valve, he passed a device that read the minutest airflow. Satisfied nothing was wrong, he put his equipment away.

He stood there rubbing his eyes and stretching with his back toward the gawking crowd. "Oh, man. . ." Cody said as he turned and saw he was being stared at. He picked up his case and his canvas and Kevlar bag put them back in the cab and locked the door. Ignoring the crowd, he spotted the Denny's across the street. Walking over, Cody could see out of the corner of his eyes they followed from a cautious distance. He wanted to put on his dark glasses to hide his eyes, and discarded the notion since his difference was obvious. Stopping to get a local newspaper from a rack in front of the restaurant, he sighed, then opened the door and walked in.

Just as he expected, everyone in the restaurant stopped what they were doing and stared, hard.

"Um, um, may I help you?" The waitress at the cash register said.

"Yes, I'd like a table, please." Cody replied.

"Um," she stammered, picking up a menu as she kept her eyes on him, "Follow me, please. . ."

Cody was a big man, standing about five eleven with dark brown hair, clean shaven. He walked with the confidence of someone who could take care of himself, and meant no harm to anyone. He sat down in the vinyl seat, picked up the menu and read it. He knew what was on it, having eaten in enough of the chains' stores on the road.

"May I take your order?" The young lady who replaced the woman from the register asked. She tried not to make it so obvious she was staring.

Cody looked up at her; Young, pretty and very nervous. "Why don't you ask me the questions?" He said.

She looked around at the restaurant's other occupants. They were looking at her with "go on, ask!" in their eyes, "Are those arms for real?"

"Yes they are."

"Where are you from?"

"Town called Four Corners."

"Are you an alien?"

"No, I'm a native."

"Wait a minute mister. Don't anybody around here look like you." A man from the next table said.

"I mean I was born here, my parents are just like you." Cody told them. "What I am is a genetic accident. A mutant..."

"You mean like the X-MEN?" one excited boy asked.

"Yeah," Cody smiled. "Only my mutation was caused by chemicals, not radiation."

"Chemicals?" the waitress asked.

"We're still working on what kind and why it happened. But apparently, a lot of toxins got together in the river near my town, and we didn't have the filters that could catch them to keep them from getting to my parents and changing them. So when my mother gave birth, I was the result." He held up his arms, and the waitress touched one of them, then put her pad down and examined the other three. "I'm more scared of you than you are of me."

The waitress let go of his hands. "I don't see how. . ."

Cody smiled. "Think about it. In a room full of people who don't look like me, I'm the one most likely to be killed if someone put their mind to doing so."

"You mean to tell me you think we'd kill you?" The man who spoke earlier said. "I don't think you're even interested in us."

Cody gave silent thanks and said; "Exactly. All I want is some breakfast."

"What would the government say if they knew about you?" A woman asked. "Would they take you away?"

"Most likely," said Cody. "You have to remember, their first job, after getting taxes is to protect you."

A little boy walked up to him and picked up an arm and turned it over in his hand. Cody's hands were calloused but clean. The child put his hand against Cody's and gave a silent "wow". He looked over at his brother who joined him, measuring their hands against Cody's. "You got big hands, mister." The first boy said.

"Did you drive that truck?" The other boy asked, pointing to the battered big rig.

"Yes, I did. I hit a slick patch the other night and I was found unconscious. That's why I was in the hospital. They didn't want to let me go." He winked at the boys. "In any case, I still want to eat." He looked up at the waitress. "Could I have four pieces of fried chicken, hash browns, and two tall stacks of pancakes, coffee, and a big glass of orange juice? This is gonna be a long day."

The waitress wrote the order down, and then went to give it to the kitchen.

The younger boy stared at Cody's eyes. "You got two, two. . ."

"Pupils," finished Cody.

"Yeah. . ." the older boy joined his brother in looking deep into Cody's eyes.

"I bet you can see real good," The older boy said.

"I've got very good night vision. I can even drive without lights. But I don't."

The boys' father got up and stared in Cody's eyes and the four armed man prayed the man wasn't the panicky type.

Or scared for his boys...

"Mister, ain't you scared to be here?" He asked.

"Only if you're scared that I am here," Cody said. "I don't hurt anybody unless they're trying to hurt me. I can understand you're being scared, I'd be scared too if I didn't know what I was looking at, and I didn't know what it was. Like I said, I don't want or need to hurt anybody unless they're trying to hurt me."

"Are you real strong mister?" The younger boy asked.

"I'm strong enough to do what I got to do," answered Cody.

"Well, I gotta tell you, I'm glad I ain't you," The father said.

"So am I. I like me just the way I am," said Cody.

"Why?" asked the older boy. "Why do you like yourself the way you are? I would be scared people would be afraid of me."

"Why do you think, until the accident last night, I hid what I was? I am scared. I see how people treat each other; so many are afraid of difference that they'll kill to keep from having to deal with it."

"You don't think much of people, do you?" A woman asked.

"Let's just say, I think the jury's still out for now." Cody replied.

"Well, least there's still hope for us, y'all. . ." she said.

"Seriously, though. I'm not gonna hold my breath. Just treat people the way I want to be treated and hope for the best." said Cody as his food arrived. He looked at the two boys and gently took his hands away from them. "If you don't mind, I'm gonna eat." Picking up his knife and fork, he said a quick prayer, than dug in.

As Cody had breakfast, keeping an eye on his truck, Dane Taylor was on the phone to his superiors. "I must admit, sir that I didn't think that the truck would hold up under that kind strain. They do build their trucks well. . Yes, sir, I know sir. . There will be an investigation. . .I don't think we can keep it a secret, sir. . .He's having breakfast, sir, right now at a Denny's. . .No, sir, I don't think there's any way we could have kept him from doing it, sir. . .He still is an American, sir. . .No sir, I don't think I just made a joke, sir. . .We've examined the truck and found it isn't leaking sir. . .Yes, the contents are still intact. . .We will question him, sir. . .Yes, I've sent a team to his hometown. . .No, I haven't opened that file yet. . .Well, sir, it hasn't arrived sir. . ."

Just then, a knock came at Taylor's hotel door.

"Excuse me, sir; I have to answer the door. . ."

Taylor went to the door, opened it and saw a Federal Express man standing there. "Are you Mister Dane Taylor?"

"Yes, I am."

FedEx handed him a clipboard. "Sign here, sir."

Taylor did so, and FedEx handed him a thick next day envelope. "Thanks." Taylor said as he closed the door, and then went back to the phone.

He fumbled with the receiver, then got it in the crook of his neck and clamped down on it. "Sir?. . .Yes, it's just arrived. . .I didn't know that we knew about this town in sixty eight. . .I understand sir, that this would be need to know. . .We can't keep this silent any more sir, and there's no way that Macabee will keep quiet. . .I think even now he's talking to people, there's no way for him to avoid it, especially if he wants to stay alive. . .I realize that sir, but the media will get to him, and that town. . .I would suggest that we don't try to keep it quiet or deny anything, we just don't act as if the sky's falling. . . We might keep this to a reasonable roar. . .I agree, sir, just get him not to panic the people. . .but haven't they cleaned that river up. . .The lab boys think chemicals may have spread beyond Four Corners? . . I don't see how, if that earlier guess about the mutagenic agents being in the water was correct, they must have found some counter agent years earlier. . .if they have, we want it. . .I understand, sir, I'll try to keep it from going too crazy sir,. . .I'll contact you when I get to Four Corners, sir. . .Right, sir. . .We'll be walking on broken glass on this one, sir. . .Good bye, sir."

Dane hung up the phone and opened the package, knowing he had an almost impossible task.

How do you keep people from finding out about something they already know?

You don't.

Dane Taylor threw the package on his bed in disgust. His superiors wanted Four Corners to be a secret again. That wasn't going to happen, and he knew it.

Didn't they handle the aliens in Northern California?

Yeah, right. Just about everyone lost their minds about that, and the alien leader really didn't give a damn one way or the other. What did Braanon Mark say?

Panic all you want, just don't bring it to our town.

Four Corners would never be the same.

From what he could see of Cody Macabee, he wasn't afraid to look you in the eye and tell you the truth, no matter how mad it made you.

Cody Macabee.

That's it.

Cody Macabee was the key to this whole thing.

Let Cody be Cody, and the rest would take care of itself.

Wait a minute.

That was it again.

Let the media try and get the boy's goat. Macabee was cool under fire, wasn't he?

Taylor breathed a sigh of relief as realized he didn't have to do anything. The people of Four Corners would take care of everything.

He hoped.

Joyce Madisen finished her stand-up report and handed the microphone to Phil Trank, her soundman. Jack Wesley, her cameraman, packed the camera away as she looked over her notes. It was three days since she woke up dazed and confused about what happened to her in Georgia, and she didn't like the mystery.

"Hey, Joyce, are you still thinking about what happened to you on your vacation?" Phil asked.

"Is it obvious?" she asked.

"Yeah, I think so." replied Phil. "You probably don't remember because you were having such a great time, and you indulged for the first time in your life."

She gave him a dirty look. "Right, Phil. Just because you don't think you've partied until you passed out. . ."

"Au contrary, MA Cherie." Phil said. "I haven't touched a drink in months."

"He's got you there, Joy." Jack said. "When you think about it, you got to admit, it's pretty funny. You pass out. I think maybe you did party a little too hard with some guy you met, and he was all over you like he had four arms. A lot of girls complain about that."

"Your sensitivity makes me gag, guys." Joyce said as she got into the van. Chuckling, the two men got in with her. "You know I don't drink."

"Hey, hey, hey; you know we're only kidding." Jack said.

"Yeah," Phil added. "Come on, I believe you."

"What?" Joyce said.

"Yeah, I believe you." Phil continued. "I did some research about that area, 'cause you got me interested. Turns out, in the fifties, there were rumors of odd births happening in that town you went through. . ."

"Four Corners . . .?" She asked.

"Yeah," continued Phil. "Rumors only. Seems they had a rash of child deaths for about a year, and then they stopped. If what you saw was true, then they've been hiding something from the rest of the country."

"Wait a minute, hiding something?" Jack asked. "What?"

"Remember when I said there was a rash of child deaths?" Phil said.

"Get to the point." Joyce said, impatient.

"Well, think about this. Supposing there was a string of births of kids with what you saw, Joyce. If the town panicked for a short time, and then decided that they couldn't afford to keep killing those kids every time one was born, they might decide that they would face it and raise these kids in secret." He picked up his bag and pulled out a thick folder. "Praise be for the freedom of information act."

"What is this?" Joyce asked. Jack was trying to see what she'd been handed and drive at the same time. "Jack, drive!" She told him.

"Okay, okay! Tell me what's in that. . ." Jack told her.

"The juicy stuff's on top." Phil said. "About the Vietnam war. . ."

There was silence as Joyce read the top papers. "Holy shit..!"

"Whoa! Invective . . .!" Jack said. "It must be hot!"

"Read it, or Jack will crash us." Phil said.

"According to this, Four Corners has four armed people living there!"

Jack stopped the van short and turned to face her. "WHAT..?..!"

"Four armed people!" Joyce summarized as she read along. "Turns out there were an unusual amount of student deferments for a town of its size. It also used medical and religious exclusions, but it was the sheer number of student deferments that caught the army's eye. They investigated and reported back. It was decided that they would help the town keep its secret, IF they would allow the government one hundred of their young men for a special unit in the war . . . oh my God. Twenty were killed. But the government kept on demanding favors for keeping quiet. Apparently they were so scared of what would happen if the general public found out, they kept the deal up." She looked up at her co-workers. "So I wasn't crazy."

"No you weren't." Phil said. "The thing about it is that they're so good at hiding in plain sight, the government doesn't even bother to enforce the deal any more. They don't need to."

Silence enfolded the van as they tried to grasp the implications. Jack started the van again and drove to their next assignment, and they all knew that something was about to break.

It broke the next morning as Joyce got up to watch the morning news. There he was her proof of sanity; Cody Macabee, big as life, and surrounded by the curious and confronted with a camera.

Joyce listened as the interview happened.

They were in a restaurant, and Cody had a cup of coffee before him.

The accident had happened the day before yesterday.

Whoever the interviewer was, Joyce hated her. This was Joyce's story, and now she would only be one of many lemmings running down there to get stories. She hated being part of the second wave.

"This is Maggie Hampton with a most unusual young man, Cody Macabee. As you can see, Cody has four arms, and if we can get a little closer. . "

The cameras zoomed in for a close up of the double pupil eyes, the pupils lay side by side, and both were a rich sky blue; then the camera zoomed back to get full shot of the two seated at the coffee shop table. Cody was still in the town the truck was in, but the tanker was long gone. Happily, the relief crew had gotten the tanker to the reclamation site before the camera crews got here.

Cody had his instructions. Be cordial, be polite, and for heaven's sake, try not to go off on stupid questions.

"My first question is, why didn't we know about you?"

Cody smiled and said; "Didn't want you to."

"You didn't want us to?"

"Course not."

"Hold it. You're saying that your people are afraid of us?"

"Oh, yeah,"

"How do you know what might happen if nobody knows you're there?"

"We just thought better safe than sorry." Cody told her, taking a sip of coffee.

Maggie gave nervous laugh. This guy was cagey, and they could see it. "Aren't you afraid of being out then?"

"Well, there's nothing I can do about it, is there?"

"How long has your town kept its secret?"

"Since the fifties…"

"The fifties..? That means that just about everyone less than fifty years old is like you."

"Yes it does." Cody told her. He enjoyed seeing the expression on her face. "Oh, don't look like that," he said with proper exasperation, "this is not bad horror movies, this is a bunch of people who found themselves with mutant kids and tried to cope with it the best they could. That look on your face is the main reason we kept our mouths shut. Who needs some news reporter causing a panic that'll level the town? I sure don't."

Maggie regained her visible composure nicely. She was amazed as to how well this, for lack of a better word, freak read her like a book. She was on the verge of panic, and he knew it.

"Right now, I can see it," Cody was saying, "All the mothers across the country using me as a bogey man to scare children into behaving; Hollywood rushing to make bad movies about us and freaked out congressmen looking to find some way of regulating us, and the really freaked out wacko wanting to kill us. Frankly, I'd rather you thought you were seeing things."

Maggie Hampton could see the sadness in his eyes that bordered on anger. "I don't know if all that would happen. . ."

"History is a nasty proof of the species, and I want to get back home in order to defend it, if necessary."

"Are your parents four armed?"

"No, they've got two. After my brother, they decided to not have any more children." He looked directly at her.

Maggie didn't betray her relief. Cody had to admire her control. It didn't excuse the thought she had of why weren't the children abortions, or why didn't they not have children at all?

Maggie could see her thoughts were all over her face, and cracked an excellent, phony smile. "Well, that all the time we have for our interview, Cody, thank you for your time."

"No, thank you. You've been most enlightening." Cody gave as phony a smile as she did.

Then the lights went off.

Cody got up, went outside and was met by Dane Taylor. "Not now, I've trying to lose a headache."

"What are you talking about?" Taylor asked.

Maggie Hampton stormed out of the coffee shop and got right in front of Cody. "How dare you!"

"How dare me what?" asked Cody.

"Make a fool out of me on camera." She said.

"You're in television. You're already a fool." Cody said.

"Well at least I'm not a freak!" She shouted, and then slapped him. Unknown to her, her cameraman, knowing his field reporter, pointed the camera at her. She was live and going to New York and across the country.

Cody had spotted the cameraman and took the blow while keeping his hands behind his back. "At least I'm not a bitch on permanent PMS." Cody walked off leaving the fuming Maggie shouting obscenities at him.

"What was that about?" Dane asked.

"An attempt to make me look bad for her own good." replied Cody.

"Didn't work, did it?" Asked Dane with a smile, realizing he'd just seen the best part of the interview.

"No it didn't," said Cody, his voice ice. "It's just the beginning, though, and I still have to wait until my team gets back so we can haul the tractor back."

"Why didn't they just take it with them? You could have been gonna long before now," asked Taylor.

"I get orders just like everyone else. Right now my job is to diffuse the situation as best I can. We don't need any morons coming to town and getting crazy."

"Don't you think that's a little paranoid?"

"It's not your behind about to get kicked," answered Cody. "I'm staying with my rig until my team comes back for me."

"That could be hours." Dane told him. "Couldn't you make other arrangements?"

Cody looked at his watch. "They should be back for me by this afternoon, around two, two-thirty. I should be all right until then."

"Right. . ." Taylor said. "Look, let me take you to a safe place. You can lock the tractor down and come back for it then."

"You gonna interrogate me?" asked Cody.

"If you'll just answer a few questions. . ." Taylor told him.

"What the hell? It's not like I'm going anywhere. . ." sighed Cody. He went to the cab and got out his bags, then locked the cab as best he could, since the window was broken. He gave small prayer the tractor would be safe, and then got into the waiting car that Dane was standing next to.

It was a long, rough day, and he hadn't finished breakfast more than a few hours ago.

6. SCUMBLE DOWN

Joyce Madisen read over the reports that had stacked up in front of her. Ever since Cody Macabee had been revealed she realized she hadn't dreamed what she seen. The people of Four Corners had no wish to be known, and as far as they were concerned, the rest of the world could stay away.

She, Jack Westly and Phil Trank were in Four Corners like everyone else in the news media, or so it seemed.

Too bad none of the townspeople were cooperating.

It seemed since the cover was blown, the townspeople took off the restraints and walked around in full four-armed glory. They went around their daily business, treating the constant questions both stupid and profound with the same basic respect. That is to say, none at all...

There was the reporter who wanted to know if having four arms improved a couple's sex life. They looked around the house at their six children and said; "Nope, not at all."

To the question if they thought that God was punishing them for any past sins, one of the first replied; "If he is, this is a strange way to do it. I'm in no pain."

Then again, there was the reporter who wanted a young man to come on his show and reveal the dark side of being four armed.

His reply..? "You're it."

In short, they went on as before, treating the extreme (some towners felt excessively stupid) curiosity about them as a cross they had to bear.

There was one reporter they didn't treat with disrespect. She was a fifteen year old girl by the name of Molly Morgan, who thought about what she wanted to ask before she asked it.

The townspeople talked with her, showed her around and generally treated her with respect.

This did not make any of the adult reporters very happy.

In the coffee shop across the street from the gas station, three reporters were talking.

Hal Porter, from Seattle, who was hoping this, would make a national name for him, stared in his cup of coffee unhappily. "You know, I'm amazed that we can't get to first base with these people. You'd think they'd want to be on television! I mean, come on! It's not like we have a disease!"

Jane Cryer, out of Chicago, dumped two packets of Sweet'n'Low in her coffee that the morning shift waitress, Hanna placed in front of her. "I was talking to one of the youngsters, and I must have said something he thought was really stupid, because he stopped talking to me, spat on the ground in front of me, got on his bike and rode away. I went back to the tape to see what I said, and I thought the question was legitimate."

"What did you ask?" Foster James, out of Atlanta, asked as he lifted a fork loaded with pancakes and syrup.

"I asked if he thought that the town should be quarantined because of what happened to it." Cryer said.

"How old was he?" Foster asked.

"Oh, about eighteen," She replied.

"There's your problem." Porter said.

"What's that?" She asked.

"They were already quarantined." Foster said. "And they liked it."

"He's got a point." Porter said. "These people have been dealing with this thing for thirty years without us coming in here and trying to save them. I think that's where we've blown it."

"You mean acting like we're here to rescue them?" Cryer asked.

"Yeah," Porter said.

Silence.

Hanna came over with Cryer's order. "Your problem is you think y'all got the answer to everything. I wouldn't talk to y'all, either. My husband had to grab this one fool and throw him in the dirt where he belonged. This may surprise you, but other people can handle difficult things without your so-called help. We been dealing with this for a long time now, and I think we have a pretty good handle on it."

Jane Cryer looked at the name tag again. "Hanna, is it? I just want to know something. Why didn't you tell anybody?"

Hanna laughed. "I was born in the fifties, honey, at the height of communist hysteria. The last thing we needed was for somebody to come around here using us as some kind of proof that the communists were out to destroy us. At least that's what my daddy told me. I had the feeling no one wanted to have us taken away from them, no matter how we looked. Anything else you want?"

"How did you cope?" Foster asked, hoping the waitress would be kind enough to keep talking.

"Honey, we just did." Hanna said. "Now if y'all don't want anything else, I got other customers."

Cryer dug into her food, a thoughtful look on her face. Foster and Porter had the same look. They needed to rethink their approach to this entire story.

"You know what I think?" Jack said as they walked around the closely-knit town looking at all the houses. "We try to make these guys look like some kind of alien monsters or something like that, and the town may kill us."

"Yeah, we all saw what happened to Tony Sexton." Phil said as he kept looking through his camera's viewfinder.

Tony Sexton was a loud, obnoxious New York television host who had promised his viewers he would get to the bottom of the story.

Mike Conners, the mayor of Four Corners invited Sexton in. Not that he wanted to, but he had to start somewhere, and Sexton's show was not syndicated to their area, and cable hadn't been laid in.

"Mr. Mayor, let's get right to the point. Your town has hidden the fact that just about all of the inhabitants is four armed for a long time. Why?" Sexton asked, assuming his usual lean into the interviewee stance.

Conners didn't like him already. "We did to protect ourselves."

"Protect yourselves? From whom?" Sexton asked.

"Protect ourselves from people who might exploit us, or worse yet, fear us." Conners said.

"Don't you think the normal people of this country have a right to know if someone like you is in their fair land?" Sexton asked.

"I was born here like everyone else." replied Conners.

"I'm sure you were. Tell me something. Do you think you might consent to an operation to make yourself normal?"

"Define 'normal'."

"Like me. Like any other human being."

"Since when were you ever that high on the food chain..?"

"I'm talking about being two armed."

"I know what you're talking about."

"Then you admit it may have crossed your mind?"

"No, it has not."

Sexton's producer could see the Mayor was beginning to get angry. This was how Tony always got his best stuff. Of course it did get him into a lot of fights, hence the three times broken nose. But Tony could have cared less, he was in his element and he knew the next few minutes were going to get him some great footage, if it didn't kill him first.

"You can't tell me you haven't wanted to leave the town and go out among regular people."

"I've done it more times than I can count."

"When..?"

"When have I gone out of town?" Conners said. "I've been around the world three times, I've gone to Japan four times and I speak Japanese, German and French."

"I'm sure that's impressive to somebody."

"It is to the Japanese, Germans and French. You haven't been out of the country in your life, and Tijuana doesn't count."

"Do you think you're superior to anyone?"

"You . . ."

Sexton stopped cold for a moment and glared at Conners, who gave him a frozen gaze.

"I don't know who you think you are mister," Conners said finally, "but I think you overstayed your welcome."

"Hold on a minute! You owe the people of this country----"

"Who the hell do you think you are? You represent nobody but yourself, and that's it, you self-serving jackass!" Conners got up, opened the door, and gestured with his two right arms. "You can leave now."

Sexton wasn't shocked, but he worked up a good head of righteous indignation and said; "You can't run away from me! And I will find out the truth!"

Conners was calm as he went to the man and gripped Sexton's right arm and lifted him to his feet. "Mister Tony Sexton, I hope you don't have any children. I'd hate to see you make the same mistake your parents did. Now get out."

Sexton started to say something, but the look on Conners face told him his next words could be his last for a long time.

Conners watched with satisfaction as Tony Sexton left. "What an ASSHOLE." He said to his secretary; "If they ain't from the networks, I don't want to hear from them, got that?"

"So they will," Francine said as she went to her desk and gave him a small glass of water that had a white powder dissolved in it.

"My B.C.?"

"Your B.C."

"Thanks." He said, and then drank it down.

"That in your face idiot deserved it. Telling the mayor he was hiding something from him and lying to America; like he was it."

They laughed as they made their way down the main street of town. Four armed children played tag, running in and out of the street. Adults stood talking with each other, going about their daily business. They seem relieved to be able to have all limbs out. Some stood with the upper arms folded, and the lower arms in their back pockets if they had pants, or hanging at their side. It was a typical small town atmosphere, and it was driving the out of town media crazy.

"I wonder how they think of all of us." Jack asked as he set the camera down for a moment on a stone fence.

"Most likely wish we'd all just go away." Joyce said, sitting on the stone fence. "I would."

"Well, they're known now, and that won't ever change." Phil said as he watched a ball bounce toward him having been kicked out of bounds by an impromptu game of kickball. A four-armed youngster ran up to them and said, "Sorry, mister." He then kicked the ball back to his friends who waited until their companion joined them.

The three New Yorkers watched as the game got back underway and realized the people of this town was going on with their lives despite whatever came their way.

Joyce turned to her crew and said; "let's go to the library and see if they have a town history. That's where we go to start."

"Finally, we're making sense." Phil said as Jack hefted the camera and they followed her.

Once inside the library, Joyce, Jack and Phil went to the card file and searched for the town's newspaper listings.

"What are we looking for?" Phil asked.

"I think it would be obvious." Jack said. "We're looking for the newspapers of thirty to forty years ago to see what they were saying about the first mutated children that were born."

"He's right." Joyce said as she went to the current newspaper to see what it was called. "I can't believe we spent all this time here and didn't even learn the name of the local newspaper."

"I guess the mayor was right. We are a bunch of self-serving assholes." Phil said, digging deeper into the card file.

Joyce went to the front desk and asked the librarian, Darlene, if there were any microfilm files of the local newspaper.

Darlene assessed her. "Don't tell me you're doing research about us?"

"Yes, we are." Joyce said.

"Well, that's a first. You want to learn what you're talking about." Said Darlene as she got up, gestured to Joyce to follow her. Darlene led the way down a set of stairs, along a long hallway, two rights into another hallway, then into a well-lit room that had several microfilm readers. It was large, clean, and Joyce could feel the flow of air as she entered behind the robust black woman. Darlene hadn't said a word as the lights automatically came on as they entered the room.

Darlene went to a stack of drawers that were labeled "FOUR CORNERS CHRONICLE" and pulled out a drawer. "This is from the late forties to the early sixties." She said in a calm voice. "You really want to know about us? This is where you start." She stepped away from the reporter and went to another drawer. "This is the local black newspaper, THE TIMES. If you're interested, the mutations were happening to the blacks in town first, around forty-five. The whites didn't feel the effects until two years later."

Joyce was shocked. "Why?"

"The water system caught enough of the mutagenic to delay the effects for two years. Blacks drew their water straight from the river because the town didn't lay pipe to us until they got theirs in first, of course. Don't you know anything about history?"

"Yes, I do." Joyce was defensive.

"Not from where I'm standing, girl," Darlene said. "If you want copies, let me know. When you're done, put everything back, and follow the arrows out. The lights will turn off by themselves." She left Joyce alone.

Joyce stared at the door long after Darlene left. She thought about the barely veiled hostility she'd felt from the woman. Not just her, but every reporter who came into town expecting a freak show, then getting frustrated when the towns' people didn't jump through hoops for them.

Joyce knew the answers were here, but it would take a long time to get to the bottom of this.

She started digging.

The trucks were still going to the disposal site. It was a set of low white building that handled toxic waste. It was a facility the rendered the potential hazardous waste inert. For twenty-five years, it was the place that local manufacturers sent what they couldn't get rid of themselves.

There were five of the buildings, and all were tightly patrolled with cameras and guard dogs watching the place.

Like the town, the people who worked there were four armed, and like the town, they kept their secrets.

Thirty years of study, thirty years of learning how chemicals could affect the human body.

Thirty years of keeping secrets.

Now that was over.

Inside the buildings, computers monitored the entire process. The humans who watched the computers double checked everything, and made sure of the purity of the inert material. The results went into landfills and building materials. It was a valuable source of income for a town that needed the money. All that research and development of the why of the mutations was expensive, and the long-term investment was paying off.

The town's doctors had become respected experts in their varied fields, and they led the way in finding the cause and prevention of birth defects. The town became renowned for the learning they did in all areas of biology. It had amazed people that they could do so much while hiding a great secret about the town.

It was a little more than frightening for some.

Harley Naismith drove his big rig, singing with the song on the radio. It was dark and his upper arms kept time with the music as his lower set were kept on the steering wheel.

Suddenly, a stopped car came into view on his headlights, and he downshifted allowing the rig to slow down, then came to a stop.

Harley got out of his truck, taking a flashlight with him. He approached the stopped car with slow, deliberate steps. As he came closer, he could see the car's glass was broken, and his innate caution warned him to get back in the truck, report the accident and drive away. But his curiosity got the best of him and he came closer to the vehicle. As he pointed his flashlight's beam into the car, he stared at the carnage that lay inside.

His repulsion drove him away from the car, and Harley turned to leave, and ran right into a shotgun pointed at his head. The redheaded Harley looked right into the barrel and said; "I just found the car like that. Whoever's in there was dead already. . ."

"You hear that, boys? The freak says he found them like that!" The shotgun's owner laughed as several figures came from behind cover, various weapons pointed right at the four-armed trucker.

Harley knew he was suckered into investigating the crash. "What do you want with me?" He pointed the flashlight at the shotgun and saw the face. Hard, cruel, there was a combination of emotions, but the one Harley could see most was fear. The shotgun wielder let him swing around to see the faces of the men who held guns on him. Shotgun was the leader, and Harley knew he was in trouble. They all had him dead to rights.

"What do you want?" Harley asked.

"Hear that, boys? The freak wants to know what we want!" Shotgun said.

"I haven't done anything to you." Harley said, trying to keep the fear out of his voice.

"Kind of shame, something like this is running around." One of shotgun's companions said. "My kids are frightened of you freak. They think you want to hurt them."

"Look, I don't even know who you people are!" Harley said trying to move so that he could make some kind of defense. He knew he was going to die, but he would try to take some of them, at least just one of them with him. "Are you that scared of me that you'd kill me just because I'm alive?" He found the hidden knife he kept up his sleeve.

"You don't get it do you, freak? You ain't natural!" Shotgun said, taking aim at his lower right arm. "We're gonna solve your little problem now."

Harley's hand flicked out and the palmed knife found shotgun's throat. Harley lunged for the weapon as it fell and turned it on shotgun's friends and fired. He hit two of the five, but was hit twice in the upper left arm. He landed near shotgun and pulled the knife from the dead man's throat. Another approached him, and Harley flicked the knife again and found that man's eye. Again he lunged for the fallen man's gun, this one a forty-five automatic, and fired it at the last two men who fled, firing shots at him. He caught a slug in the leg.

"Lord, why me?" He asked rhetorically as he crawled over to the corpse and pulled the knife from his eye. He ripped a piece of cloth with it from his shirt and tied a tourniquet around his leg. He did the same with his arm. He rested for a few minutes, then wrapped his hands in cloth torn from the body of shotgun, then cleared the weapons from the bodies, putting them in his truck. They would be disposed of when he got to the disposal site. He went back to the bodies, pulled their wallets and placed them in the truck with the weapons. He pulled the corpses in line with the wheels of the truck, limped back, climbed painfully into the rig, started her up, and then ran over the corpses as he drove away.

7. BROTHERLY LOVE

If nothing else, the last few days since the discovery of the town of Four Corners, Mac and Ronald Dennison found they rather liked the new found notoriety of their home. It didn't mean they approved of everything that happened, but they liked that they could now have all four arms out in the open and not too many people would comment on it.

"How you doing', Marcy..?" Mac said as he and his brother sat in their usual booth and ordered their usual Sunday morning breakfast of ham, southern style hash browns, biscuits and gravy, with black coffee and big glasses of juice. Ronald liked fresh orange, while Mac took fresh grapefruit.

They notice Marcy handled more orders now that she could handle more than two or three plates at a time. "Looks like they doing more business these days, don't it?" Mac said as they watched the woman take orders and deliver the food to waiting tables with her customary efficiency.

"Yeah, it must be a little hard for her nowadays. I hope John gets her some help." Ronald said as he sipped from his glass of juice.

"Hey lady, we know you've only got four arms, but we're waiting!" The young man who said that was about twenty, dressed in torn jeans, a leather jacket and dark glasses with dirty blond hair and an attitude.

"I just took your order, and it'll be up in a few minutes, unless you like it raw." Marcy said, not liking the kind of curiosity seekers that were coming around since the revelation. It hadn't made Marcy any happier she had to deal with the sort of idiots who had no respect for any one, let alone people like her.

The boy didn't seem to notice where he was, nor did he seem to care. He was out for a good time, and he didn't seem to care if the people in the coffee shop thought him a fool.

Then he got stupid. As Marcy passed by, he grabbed her arm, and she nearly dropped the tray of food she carried. "Look, you freaky bitch," he said as he pulled her closer, "I said I wanted my food!"

"Take your hands off of me!" Marcy said as she pulled away from the boy. Her tray dropped, spilling the contents on the floor. She apologized to the table the food was meant for, but the boy pushed his luck.

He kicked her when she bent over.

Mac and Ronald glanced at each other, then got up and went to the boy's table. "Think you ought to apologize to the lady." Mac said calmly as his body went to a ready stance.

"You know, this ain't your town, boy. And it ain't nice to pick fights with strangers." Ronald said.

"This is none of your business, freak!" The boy said pulling a knife and waved it at the two four armed men. His friends looked worried, and two others pulled knives.

"Look at this . . . they got knives, Mac." Ronald said.

"They do at that. How do you feel about that?" Mac asked.

"Scares me bad, brother," Ronald replied.

"Me, too," Mac said. "What say we do something about it?"

"Now I agree with that." Ronald said as he moved quicker than the out of towners thought they could and grabbed the boy's knife arm and twisted it behind his back.

His brother moved faster than he did, disarming the other two and grabbing them. "Somebody want to help us?" Mac asked. Two other four armed men got up and picked the youngsters up by their feet and carried them outside to the trash dumpster. One four armed boy opened the lid, and the knife welders were unceremoniously dumped into the garbage.

The youths got on their feet, covered with garbage, and shouted a string of curses at the top of their lungs. Their friends made frantic efforts to free them from their humiliating position.

"Parents shouldn't have children if they ain't got the time to raise them." Mac said.

"Better yet, they should be sterilized. The kids, I mean." Ronald said.

Marcy gave them all free pie after they washed up and sat back down.

"You know that's just the first of that kind of thing to happen." Marcy said.

"No it ain't." Bill Tupper said, as he took his pie ala mode.

"What are you talking about?" Mac asked, puzzled.

"You haven't heard about Harley Naismith?" Tupper asked. "He was attacked on his way to the disposal unit, northeast of town. Killed three, and scare off the other two. Came in limping; now, I'm gonna tell y'all something, you didn't hear it from me."

"How do you know about it?" Mac asked dropping his fork in surprise.

"I came into the section head's office as Harley was giving his deposition. I wasn't supposed to hear it, of course, but I couldn't help it."

"Well, that just floats my boat." Marcy said.

"More like a sinking ship." Ronald said.

"Hey, Tup. You think the mayor's gonna order two men to every shipment of the waste? You know we've been talking 'bout that for years. Now that we're known, we ought to double up just to be on the safe side." Mark Hamer said. "I got to tell you, now that outsiders know about us, I'm nervous about making a drop by myself."

Jack Weaver spoke up. "Don't blame you, Mark. I don't mind making the runs if I'm sure I'll get there. Do you know what some wacko could do with that stuff?" He shook his head. "I don't even want to think about it."

"Jack, just because we're known now, doesn't mean anyone will attack you, me or anybody else." Mac said as he glanced out the window. He smiled. "I see the sheriff and two of his deputies have helped those fools we put in their proper place." He laughed. "The deputies are makin' sure they get in their car and out of town!"

The coffee shop roared with laughter, except for two two-armed people who didn't think it was funny at all.

"I think you're horrible for laughing at them. They were only children!" The woman said, angry.

"Who might you be ma'am?" Bill Tupper asked.

She looked at her husband, and then said: "I'm Helen Morgan, and this is my husband David."

"Well, Mrs. Morgan, you've got to understand something. One, that boy is out of control. Two, he's just found out nobody has to take what he was dishing out. Three, I'm sorry if you feel that way, but, Marcy didn't deserve what he did to her. Now I don't know how your people are where you come from, but here in Four Corners, we look after each other. You ain't gonna do it, the government ain't gonna do it. If we let people walk all over us just because of what we are and the way we look, well, we'd be dead pretty soon. And we kinda like who and what we are. I'm afraid if you don't like it, you're gonna have to leave. This is our town, and we will defend it."

Helen and her husband, David looked around the coffee shop and saw the hard, determined looks on their faces. The two normal realized something that the youngsters who had been thrown out didn't: in this town, it was normal to have four arms, not two. Anybody not a parent of one of these people, were just tourists. "I'm very sorry." She said nervously. "I just realized what you mean."

"I could understand if it was just one or two of us, but we are in the majority here." Mac said. "You just spoke as you believed, that's all. Nothin' wrong with that…"

"I guess my wife and I didn't expect what we just saw." David finally spoke. "I guess we're like everyone else coming through here, expecting to see some kind of show . . . I guess we really have something to be sorry about."

Marcy poured them both another cup of coffee. "I just wish everyone who came through here felt the way you do now. Might make it easier on everybody . . ."

"Tell me something. Do you have the same feelings we do? I mean, about love, and everything?"

"Well if we don't, I wasted my time makin' six kids!" Bill Tupper said.

"Tup, please!" Marcy said laughing. "That ain't the only thing we feel, and you know it!"

Helen blushed, and her husband joined in the laughter.

"What I really want is for people to not be scared of us. We ain't hurtin' anybody." Tupper said. "I just want have my life, here in Four Corners. There ain't anything from outside that I want."

His friends and neighbors chorused their agreement.

"Ain't anybody here your enemy," Ronald said. "We can be friends, if you want it, but you got to want it. We make bad enemies."

"I can see that." Helen said. "What are you going to do about the people that want to hurt you?"

"Hurt 'em right back if they can't be reasoned with." Mac said. "I don't like the idea of killin', but if it's to protect me and mine, then I'll do it.

Helen looked at the citizens of this town. Mac was right. This was the only place they were safe. She glanced over at the woman who served their food and saw it in her face. She looked again in the other's faces, and could see it. They would die to protect their town, and each other. "I envy you. Being this close, I mean."

"Well, ma'am, that's the way it has to be." Ronald said. He looked at his watch. "We'd better get going, brother. We got that load to haul this afternoon."

Cody Macabee walked down the hall of the hospital clad only in his pants. Since he didn't wear underwear, and hospital robes weren't made for his form, the pants were a reasonable compromise.

For now. . . .

Doctor Theresa St. Thomas and Doctor Thurston Harris and their team watched as Cody entered the examination room.

Cody looked around and said: "So you're the people who going to dissect me?"

Doctor St. Thomas, a stern faced, yet attractive woman in her forties with dark brown hair frowned through her glasses at him. "Mr. Macabee, I wish you wouldn't refer to these examinations as dissections. I'd like you to remember that you volunteered to do this. . . "

"Yeah, just to keep you from kidnapping one of us and ripping them apart. . ." Cody said coldly. "The fact is, I don't trust you, and I am scared shitless that you might "accidentally" kill me. So, forgive me if I would rather not know about you wanting to know all about me. I don't trust you people."

A heavy silence hung in the room for a long time before Harris spoke. "Mr. Macabee, we will not do you any harm. I want you to understand that. I wish I could say I understood your fear of us, but considering your people have kept their secrets for almost fifty years, you must recognize our apprehension."

"Apprehension at what..?" Cody said studying the man's face.

"Our apprehension that you might try to mutate other people to be like yourselves," Harris said firmly. "I think those are legitimate fears."

Cody would have spat, but he remembered his manners. "Then I was right. I'm not coming out of this alive." He looked at the other doctors and tried to keep from vomiting. He looked down at the floor and could feel his legs nearly give out from under him. "Lord, I've walked into the pit. I commend my soul unto thee. . ."

The others in the room knew Cody just gave up and wouldn't fight them.

Cody was glad he settled his affairs before coming here.

"He is walking out of here alive, isn't he?" St. Thomas asked.

"He'd better. I don't want to think what could happen if he doesn't. They protect their own." Harris said.

"But isn't that what we're trying to do; protect ourselves?" St. Thomas asked.

"Yes. But both sides don't agree on what kind of protection is necessary." Harris looked at his team, and then at Cody, who was on his knees, praying.

"My God, he's terrified!" One of the nurses whispered.

Harris looked at his team, and knew they had to use kid gloves. The young man's death could start a war.

Bodine Macabee sat on his front porch with a tall glass of lemonade. It wasn't as cool as it had been, as a matter of fact, there was an unseasonable hot spell going on.

The elder Macabee rocked back and forth as he sipped from his glass, trying not to think that his son called and asked him to take care of his earthly possessions. The whole town was expecting the same thing Cody did; he would not come out of it alive.

The thought ate at the elder Macabee like a cancer. He didn't want to think about it, and he couldn't help but think about it. Finally, he couldn't hold the glass anymore and it shattered on the porch.

Bodine Macabee went inside, got his Bible and started to read. He wanted to call a thousand curses on the people who had his son, but he couldn't. He sat there until he read the entire Bible cover to cover. He prayed, sang his favorite hymns, got on his knees, stood up, fell to his knees again.

He did this all night until he fell asleep with his head resting on the Bible. He didn't wake up until noon next day.

The town talked about the news that Cody was in the hands of two armed people. Most everyone shuddered to think that right now, he was being dissected. The fear froze the blood of most townspeople.

The trucks with the waste from the town's plants had double riders, now.

Parents refused to allow their children out after dark.

The sheriff deputized fifty more people, just in case.

After school activities were curtailed when dusk fell.

Joyce Madisen stood in front of the local teen hangout doing a stand up report.

"Behind me is the local hangout for Four Corners' teenagers. What's wrong with this picture?"

The camera panned the empty lot and the closed shop.

"No one is here to party or hang out. This is Saturday night."

Joyce walked slowly to the front door. "Until a few days ago, this was a lively, jumping place. There would be kids dancing, playing video games, and having your basic good time. But for now, that's over." She walked toward four youngsters, sitting on benches in front of the HOT AND HASTY/VIDEO ARCADE, watching her approach. She continued. "The reason is simple. One of their own is in the hands of the government. His name is Cody Macabee. . ." Cody's high school picture flashed on the screen. "He is the Four Corners man whose big rig tanker truck hit a slick patch and rolled over. Thanks to his skill in driving, a disaster was averted since the tanker truck did not spill its load of toxic waste. He was unconscious when found, and his shirt was ripped open, revealing his having been born with four arms." She came to the four youths who eyed her suspiciously, and had their arms wrapped around themselves. Two, a boy and a girl, linked arms together, trying to keep their shaking from being evident.

"Now, they won't give me their names, and I won't press them for them. But they have agreed to talk. And that may be more important than anything right now." She turned to the first boy.

"Are you afraid the same thing might happen to you?"

"Sure I am," he answered in a slight drawl, "I don't know if he's coming out alive, and I don't want the same thing to happen to me."

"Do you think it is just what the government says it is--an examination?"

"I don't know what to think." The second boy answered, "All I know is that the government's got him. That's as good as a death sentence."

"You don't believe he'll be released?"

"Please! Do you really think we're that stupid to even trust them?" The first girl answered. "The government ain't here to protect me; it's here to protect you, lady! We don't even count as a finger on an amputated hand!"

"Will life in this town ever get back to normal?"

"I doubt it," said the first boy.

"What will you do until this is over?"

"Stay undercover." The second girl said. "It's the only thing we can do, besides defending our town. I can only think there are a lot of people who are willing to kill us for being what we are."

"Do you think it would help if people knew how your mutations happened?"

"Not when you consider a senator from this state wants to sterilize us so we can't have children. We don't mean anyone any harm, so I don't know why he wants to do that."

"Yes you do," said his girlfriend. "It's like them wanting to sterilize mental patients so they won't have kids. Suppose to protect the more able people from having kids with them."

"Like we want to have children with anyone from outside, anyway," said the first girl. "They can just stay out of Four Corners, as far as I'm concerned."

"I think we ought to sue him for trying to make us the latest bogeyman so people would vote for him, as if he could protect them from us." The first boy said. "I've got no interest in leaving this town to live anywhere else. I like it here just fine."

"What really bugs me about all of this debate is that no one asked if what we thought about the whole thing. After all it affects us most of all." The first girl said.

"Do any of you believe this will come to a good end?"

A chorus of no's was their answer.

"I think there's gonna be a bloodbath before this is over." The first boy said.

"I think we're gonna have to arm ourselves because too many people are ready to kill us, right now." The second boy said. "I've been practicing. . ."

Joyce could hardly contain her shock. "You mean target practicing?"

"Best thing to do these days, especially if the rabble rousers keep it up." The second boy said. "We may not have a choice. . ."

Joyce let it hang in the air for a moment, and then turned to the camera. "As you can see, the young people of Four Corners are ready to defend themselves, if these youngsters are representative of their age group. But the fact is, the entire town is ready to do what they must if it all comes down to shooting. Joyce Madisen, WNYC News."

". . . annnnd we're out!" Jack said as he cut his camera off. We'll send this up. "I hope they don't cut it. This was too good."

"Most likely," Joyce said. She turned to her interviewees. "Thanks. You did great, especially when you opened up."

"They'll probably cut it and make us look like a bunch of blood thirsty monsters." The first boy said.

"Yeah," The first girl said as she ran her fingers through her hair. It was her nervous tick, and she was glad she didn't do it on camera. "I just want to survive this."

"Amen to that!" said the second boy. "Right now, we'd better get off the streets before our parents pitch a fit." The four youngsters walked over to a sixty-three Chevy Impala that had been restored to like new form, got in and drove off.

Joyce, Jack and Phil watched them drive off, realizing, whether they want to be or not, they were part of this whole thing.

"Guys, let's get that history finished."

8. SHELTER ME FROM FEAR

The town waited to see if Cody would come out the examinations the government was putting him through alive. The tension was high, charged and dangerous.

The Reverend Jimmy Robertson hosted a show called the Spirit Club. A two-hour talk show that had a definite religious orientation that minced no words, and cut no slack on what they thought the wrongs and sins done in the world.

He loved Four Corners.

He loved the fact that the town was the center of controversy.

He loved that he could use it for showing that Biblical prophecy was true.

Most of all, he thought he could use the town to bring more people to Christ.

He didn't ask the town what they thought, or if they believed.

Two days after the revelation Four Corners existed, he spoke about it on the show. But he was smarter than the networks. He sent people into the town to feel it out before making any kind of statement.

"You know, friends, it hurts me to think the people of the town of Four Corners felt they had to hide from the rest of the world. If they had the true faith, I think they would have found that it didn't matter if they had four arms or no arms; God loves them just the same. Now, in about a week, Spirit Club reporter Mike Crenshaw will have a report for us about the town, and he will try to find out why they felt they had to hide from the rest of the world."

Mike Conners and the Rev. Jacob McCandless, who was pastor of the Everlasting Faith Church, and the Rev. Holman

Caulder, who was pastor of the Holy Truth Baptist Church, along with three other colleagues, plus the sheriff, and several members of the town council watched in the school auditorium. They watched until the show ended.

Nobody was pleased.

"Well, I like that." McCandless said. "The man has his nerve, suggesting that we don't have 'true faith', whatever that is."

"What bothers me is that he thinks he's going to bring us to God. I think we're already there. At least, I am in no doubt about my faith, and I don't need some television preacher to tell me how to pray." Conners said as he adjusted himself on his chair. "I'm getting sick of outsiders trying to tell us how to pray. Or live."

"Personally, I resent him thinking he's going to take care of our business for us. This town does not need a nursemaid." Holman Caulder said with disgust. "I don't care to have him come here and tell us we haven't taken care of this town's spiritual needs." He wiped his dark brown face with his handkerchief. He sweated heavily, even in cold weather, and when he was in full preaching mode, was known to run a river of sweat as he broke into song in the middle of the sermon. "My friends, I think it's time we put an end to outsider notions that they are gonna save us."

"Amen to that. But you know what I think? I think we should try to meet them not with anger, we should meet them with the full glory of one of our worship services." Caulder said.

"Don't you mean full fury?" McCandless asked, mopping his brow.

"No, no, no, no. I mean full glory, in one of our usual services." Caulder said. "What we need to do is show the sort of faith that's in this town. I don't mind somebody coming in here to worship with us, but I do mind somebody telling me I don't know Jesus."

Conners looked dubious. "I don't think they're gonna fall for it."

"Who's saying anything about making them 'fall for it'? I mean showing them the truth about us!" Caulder said. "I think we ought to hold a revival meeting or meetings this week. I don't say they're gonna like what we do or how we do it, but considering that every one of us in this room is four-armed, I think it behooves us to show to the world who we are, and that they have nothing to fear." He chuckled. "Unless of course they start a fight, which no one wants?"

Wiping his hands on his pants, and then dropping his arm to his lap, Conners scanned all the faces in the room. "I don't know what you're gonna make of this, but I think Cody had the right idea. I think it dovetails right with what you're sayin', Reverend. I would rather no one knew about us. I would rather no one from the outside was here. I'm not one for makin' speeches, but here I am doin' it, fine." He stood up, stretched, looked at everyone again, and then continued. "I do not like the situation. I do not like the fact that we are seeing the looky-loos and the fools. I don't like that the media is here makin' us seem like we are the next worst thing since Hitler. I think what we ought to do is go about our lives any way, we just don't try to hide anything except our anger, if we can."

"Mike, are you saying, do nothing?" McCandless asked, "That's crazy!"

"No, it's perfect. If we do anything first, we're in the wrong. Let them make the first mistakes. Then whatever happens, we will only be defending ourselves." Conners said. "We can't be seen as the aggressors in this. All of this attention will pass. We won't be the same, but we will still be here. That is what I care about." He looked at the gathered men and women. "I'm as scared as you. But I will not be driven back into hiding because of someone else's fear. We can't go back."

McCandless and the others looked at each other not sure if they liked what they were hearing. How could they defy the entire world's curiosity?

"Mike, this will not be easy." Caulder said uneasily. "We've got to talk to the town somehow and get them to get in on this." He wiped his brow. "I want to know something. Do we defend ourselves against attack, or do we just take it?"

"Hell no..!" Jenlee Farris said. "I will rot before I let some idiot treat me like trash and get away with it! You'd best believe I would give as good as I get!" The room exploded with cheers.

Conners held up his hands. "I get the message. Just make sure that whatever you do is equal to whatever's done to you, no more than that." He searched their faces. "Is there any more business?" No one answered. "I guess that's it, let's go home."

As they stood up to leave, McCandless said; "Lord, shelter me from fear."

"Amen!" Everybody said.

9. BREAKDOWNS

Mayor Conners watched as the big tent went up in the vacant lot just outside the town limits. The uneasy feeling just would not go away, and it grew as the trucks rumbled by on their way to the disposal site.

The last thing Conners wanted was a disaster. So why was he afraid of a revival tent meeting?

Okay, so Jimmy Robertson was a nationally known televangelist. That wasn't a crime. Nor was his preaching anything to be afraid of.

But something just didn't feel right.

Conners remembered the riot at the abortion clinic two towns away. Robertson had held a series of programs talking about the evils of abortion and how these places should go down in flames.

Of course, he didn't accept the blame when an abortion clinic went up with three patients and the doctor performing the abortion died in the fire.

That he was anti-abortion didn't bother Conners; it was the way he went about it. He had no remorse for the people who died, and was quite happy when another clinic in the area closed its' doors after the doctor had been shot at.

No, it was the programs Robertson broadcast about Four Corners.

Fine, they had shown the people of the town worshiping at their churches.

They had shown everyday life in town.

The pictures didn't bother Conners as much as the voice over.

That had scared Conners.

It was about how creation didn't take in account the sort of mutations the people of Four Corners were born with, how

there could not be an allowance for the people of this town and their sin of not miscarrying when the women should have.
. .

It went on and on every day, the implication being there was something wrong in their having been born healthy despite their mutations.

Conners was scared.

He could feel the breakdown coming.

It was Saturday night.

The revival rolled into town like a holy juggernaut bent on cleaning up Hell.

The Sheriff and his deputies were armed and ready, having surrounded the tent. They kept in contact with radios and tried their best not to look scared.

The music came up with all the glory the choir and band could muster.

There were shouts of hallelujah and words of praise and fervent hand clapping and shout as the service got a full head of steam.

Then, the sermon began.

Jimmy Robertson was resplendent in beautiful white three-piece suit, and he carried a handkerchief that he waved around as the music sounded.

Mike Conners sat in the back row, sweating from the combined heat of a thousand bodies crammed into that tent. He loved the music, and they had sung some of his favorite hymns, but he could not relax.

His throat tightened as Robertson stepped to the pulpit. There were video cameras recording the meeting, since Robertson liked to have a record of his revivals. He liked to show clips on his show.

"You know, brothers and sisters, when I first heard of this town, I wondered, what was the place these people had on earth." Robertson began. He smiled hugely. "I believe I have found it in Genesis."

Here it comes, Conners thought, and I'll bet even money we aren't mentioned in there.

Robertson read the appropriate passage, and then said, "Man was created in God's image. It is not in man's hands to recreate him."

There it is, Conners thought. Now, let's see if he hangs himself. Conners knew that there were media waiting to see what the famed televangelist had to say.

Jimmy Robertson preached magnificently. He thundered he condemned the fact of this town; he condemned the fact that the children were born healthy despite their mutations, and he especially condemned what called "the selfish and unfeeling people who would perpetuate the mistakes of their parents by having more of these children who are an abomination before God."

He went on and Conners worst fears seemed to be coming true. The fervor rose, and the media spotted him, and several cameras caught his horrified expression and sent it out over their feeds.

His voice wanting to die in his throat, Conners stood up and shouted: "What are you trying to do to us?!" He screamed until he was heard over the crowd.

A spotlight glared in his face, nearly blinding him. Conners was glad he could stand the light as his double pupil eyes adjusted.

Robertson smiled a beatific smile. "Why my poor, misshapen brother; I'm just trying to bring the word to you."

"By inciting a riot . . .?" Conners stood his ground. "I've read the Bible every day of my life, and I have never read in it what you've read."

"Perhaps, you haven't read it correctly." Robertson said, holding his copy up. "I don't find that you are supposed to exist. There is not one word about four armed, double pupil eyed people in here."

"I want to know why." Asked Conners, knowing full well he was too far in the enemy camp to do much good. "There is not one man woman or child who has ever harmed you. This isn't about what's in the Bible, it's about what's in your heart. This is about your fear."

Robertson shook his head sadly. "I wish I could spend some time with you and make you understand that it would be better if this town was cleansed of its sin."

Conners closed his eyes, and let the tears come. He didn't care that the image went all over the world. He opened his eyes and said, "The devil can quote scripture, but only man can make hell on earth." He turned and left. He didn't hear Robertson's reply.

The sheriff and his men, having watched the meeting on portable televisions, met him outside the tent. "That man's crazy. . ." Mosley said as he looked back at the tent. "What's he trying to do?"

"Exactly what I think he's trying to do," Conners said, "start a war between us and the rest of the world."

"We haven't done anything to him!" Jackie Marston said. "Why does he want us dead?"

"You heard the mayor, the man is scared." Opie Richards said. "There are enough people who don't want to know we exist." He spat in the dirt. "We got to get ready."

Conners clenched and unclenched his fists, then kicked at a rock. "We got no choice, now. Get word out to everyone, get ready, dam's about to bust."

Cody Macabee's hearts beat steady as the doctors probed and poked. Hadn't they done enough retina scans, blood tests, urine and feces samples? Hadn't they enough skin and hair samples?

All this examination had gotten old real fast.

"Doc St. Thomas, aren't you done yet?" Cody asked. "I feel like a pincushion."

Theresa St. Thomas chuckled as she read the results of his electrocardiogram. "You must understand something, Cody. When I first heard of your people, I wondered why you happened."

"Really . . .?"

"Don't be sarcastic." St. Thomas said raising an eyebrow. I think you know what I mean." There were other doctors in the room and their ears pricked up and some turned to the doctor and examinee. "I think you and your people have figured out why you happened."

"How did we happen?" asked Cody knowing that after two weeks, the doctor and he had gotten on a parallel track, if not downright simpatico as the doctor made educated guesses on why they were born the way they were.

"I'd say you were supposed to be twins." St. Thomas said, as she walked around him as Cody lay on the examining table.

"What makes you guess that?" asked Cody, knowing the doctor was so very close, if not on it.

"Your two hearts, double pupils and four arms," she said, "Whatever triggered the mutations forced what should have been twin children into a being that was combination of everything. Cody, your people are a genetic accident that replicated itself. It should not have happened, but it did. Instead of the infants dying, they survived. Do you have any children?"

"Not yet, and right now I'm not too sure about it. I want kids, but I'm not married yet." Cody said shifting so he could see the doctor. They gazed at each other for a moment. "It's too bad you aren't like me."

Doctor St. Thomas swallowed nervously.

"Don't worry," Cody said calmly. "It was only a thought. Besides, the girl I love is back in Four Corners. I mean you're a good thought to have. I like you, but neither one of us is stupid."

"Why is a man with three degrees driving a truck?" One of the other doctors asked.

"Who's asking?" said Cody, who couldn't see his questioner from the table.

"I'm Doctor David Foshay."

"What's your specialty?" asked Cody.

"I'm a geneticist." Foshay said. "I understand you have a degree in genetic engineering."

"And..?"

Foshay looked around at his colleagues, and then said, "I wonder if you didn't do this to yourselves."

Cody closed his eyes and sighed. "Tell me something, Doctor. What sane human being, even under the most stupid conditions would do this to himself and his children? Do you really believe that somebody wanted to have children like me?" He cleared his throat. "The first white couple to have a baby went more than a little crazy. The father killed himself, and the mother hasn't spoken since then. Their son visits her in the mental hospital outside of Atlanta, but she doesn't see him, doesn't respond. There were several couples like that whom not only committed suicide, but also they took the baby with them. The town was so ashamed and scared of what happened, they started to work to finding out why. That's why I have my degrees: to help my people finish the puzzle." He looked at St. Thomas. "You're right, Doctor, I was supposed to be twins.

"Oh, my Lord," St. Thomas gasped. "I didn't think I was completely right. Have you figured out why?'

"The local water sources were badly polluted, especially the river were most of the town water was drawn. The blacks in town were affected first, and they hid the truth from the rest of the town for a long time." Cody said, sitting up. "When these two doctors started investigating the births, they found out the blacks were having the mutated children earlier, about 'forty-five or so. My grand dad was one of the first births. My mom and dad were of the second wave. By that time, everyone knew enough to keep their mouths shut."

"Keeping that secret for so long. . ." Foshay said. "I can imagine your fear of discovery. . ."

"But that's all you can do, Doctor. We kept silent because we didn't want any panic or somebody deciding we weren't supposed to be alive and doing something about it." Cody rubbed his eyes with the upper pair of hands as the lower propped him up. "I play a two necked guitar because I just couldn't stand not having one set of hands not do anything. I'm amazed that you haven't done any dexterity tests yet."

Foshay looked at his colleagues then gave a sheepish grin. "Hadn't occurred to us yet,"

"Now it has." Said Cody as he pulled off the sensors and stretched and yawned, then slipped his feet into his waiting slippers and put on his four-armed robe. He fixed a hard gaze on the gathered doctors. "I've got some phone calls to make, and all you've got is more of the same data. Get creative, or I'm leaving." He left.

Foshay went to St. Thomas's side. "Why didn't we think of dexterity tests?"

"I've thought of them, I just didn't think he'd mind one last round of medical scans." She shrugged. "I guess we can start with the dexterity tests tomorrow."

Foshay grinned wickedly. "I think he likes you. Maybe he wants to do an experiment in breeding. . ."

Theresa St. Thomas glared at her colleague. "You are one sick puppy." She stormed out of the examination room.

Once out of the building, Doctor St. Thomas spotted Cody as he walked the grounds, swing his arms in wide arcs, then making circles. He took off the robe and dropped down and did fifty sets of push-ups with each set of arms, first top to bottom, and then each side. She watched, fascinated as he put himself through a rigorous workout. She then heard him begin a spoken set of calculations that astounded her in their complexity. As he began, St. Thomas wrote the problems down on the back of several sheets of paper that contained her measurements from that afternoon's exams. After he finished, he sat in a lotus position, let his breathing even out and closed his eyes and went into a deep trance.

St. Thomas walked slowly toward him and circled, wanting to touch him, but holding back. Her colleagues came out to the same garden and watched the two as she circled the still four armed man. Eventually, they all joined her, quietly whispering among them about why Cody would do such a thing.

Foshay was the first to break away, taking St. Thomas by the arm, their colleagues following.

Cody opened one eye, watched as the doctors went back inside of the hospital, sighed, and then went back into his meditation.

The next day, Jimmy Robertson went out among the people of Four Corners, his entourage including a cameraman who videotaped everything.

The people of Four Corners could care less.

The comments were telling as they told him what they thought of him. Such as:

"Go back to where you came from!"

"There ain't nothing you can tell me about the Lord!"

One man spat on him and said; "We don't want your kind here! This town was a haven from thugs like you!"

"This is a Christian town, MISTER Robertson! We ain't done nothing to you, and now you've given every crazy in four states fuel for what they think they can do to us!"

There was a group of teenagers who had gotten together a bucket of fresh feces they had just passed and mixed with some horse manure. They got ahead of the now beleaguered group that was being followed by the secular media and made sure they were in the perfect position. Once the group stopped and Robertson was about the gathered people who were glaring at him with the purest contempt Robertson had ever seen directed at him. He was inwardly wishing he'd stayed in his studio, having just found out just how much he was appreciated here.

He faced the reporters and began. "I have to tell you, I can only say what I feel has been put on my heart. . ."

"Reverend . . .?" a voice came from behind him.

James William Robertson turned to respond to that voice. What he got was a barrage of feces that hit him in a brown rain. Someone had a bucket of steaming urine and threw it into Robertson's face.

The urine thrower screamed at him. "Go back to your studio, boy! We don't need you here!"

"Yeah..!" Another shouted, "You're just doing this because you're scared we want to fuck your daughter! I wouldn't touch the bitch with a ten foot pole!"

A girl screamed. "Get out of our town!"

The shout was taken up:

"GET OUT!"

"GET OUT OF OUR TOWN!"

"GET OUT YOU UNHOLY BASTARD!"

Worse was said as more feces came flying, and the media had long since given distance to the opponents as Robertson's party was covered in dark brown, foul smelling shit.

Robertson began to run, even as he slipped face first into the slippery street. An aide helped him up, and someone had brought his car around quickly, and the party piled in even as the feces still flew at them.

"Drive back to the tent!" Robertson shouted.

"Sir, I don't think we should . . ." the driver started to say.

"I didn't ask what you thought! Get us to the tent!"

The driver did as he was told.

He wished he hadn't.

Robertson's feces covered face went wide in horror as there was nothing more than smoldering ash heap left of the revival tent. The driver stopped the car, and the shocked party got out, walked around the site, mute as they realized the town would take nothing from anyone, not even a nationally known televangelist who thought their very existence was an affront to their God.

Robertson and his party climbed back in the smelly car and got out of Four Corners. He would say whatever he thought from a safe distance.

The ACLU called the actions of the town "cowardly and humiliating" to Robertson, and demanded an apology from the mayor.

The mayor replied; "Sue us, you still won't get anything but shit."

The ACLU announced they would bring a lawsuit on behalf of Jimmy Robertson Ministries, claiming their first amendment rights had been violated.

The town counter sued, saying that the televangelist had caused great mental distress, and performed an act of great mental cruelty against the town by saying they had no right to exist.

The judge threw them out of court.

10. BURNDOWN

It started simply.

It wasn't as if anyone wasn't expecting it.

It started on a Tuesday.

It wasn't as bloody as it could be.

It was a blessing more weren't hurt or killed.

It wasn't something anyone could have prevented.

It wasn't the worst that could occur, either.

It was, how could you say it? Bad enough to make you want to kill, but not so bad that you'd do it....

It was one night of a bunch of skinheads thinking they could get away with it.

It was the stupidest idea they'd ever had.

Now, it must be understood that not all skinheads are racists. For the majority in America, it is a fashion statement, an attitude.

For some, it is a way of identifying themselves as superior, of forming comradeship with their fellows. It is the so-called Aryan power movement.

Back to Sunday . . .

It was also one Peter Devires, Jr. and his friends, all bonded together in a knot of twisted ideology, warped religion, and self-delusion so massive they consider Adolph Hitler, God.

They were out to do what Jimmy Robertson couldn't do: show the world what had crawled up from hell.

Peter Devires, Jr. held the meeting at his farm in the next county.

"I think we all know why we're here?" Devires said to his followers. "I think we've all seen the freaks that have been living in the town of Four Corners for a long time, and nobody knew about it. Now, I don't know about you, but I don't think they have a right to live, period. They are a perversion of what ought to be, normal, two armed people, living lives."

The gathered crowed of about fifty men roared their agreement.

"Now, this is what I say we do: we burn that pit down and send those freaks back to hell where they belong!"

The fifty roared again, this time waving their automatic rifles in the air.

"We are gonna clean this trash from the face of the earth!" Devires said making the Nazi salute, and his followers did the same, with hearty rounds of "Heil! Heil!" Devires called for silence. "Here's how we do it. . ."

It was Monday.

Bodine Macabee sat on his front porch and rocked back and forth as he smoked his pipe and watched the Honda Accord drive up on the dirt driveway and come to a stop. The driver, a man dressed in a gray, rumpled suit and his passenger, a woman in a beige business suit got out and walked up to the porch. "Are you Mr. Bodine Macabee?"

"Who are you, and why would you want to know?" answered Bodine as he relit his pipe. "If y'all 'lergic to pipe smoke, too bad. This is my house."

"We're from the IRS, Mr. Bodine. We're investigating the residents of Four Corners past tax returns."

"I'd like to know why." Bodine said, raising an eyebrow. "I'm paid up and legal. Besides, why should I talk to people who ain't got no names?"

The two IRS agents shrugged their shoulders, pulled out their identification. Bodine took them and read them. "Mary Washington, Jeff Kincaid." He handed the ID's back to them. "Well, Mary, Jeff, what can I do for you?"

"Like I said, we're just checking out the town's tax returns. . . ." Kincaid started.

"I still don't understand why?" Bodine said. "The only thing we hid from outsiders was the fact we had four arms. There ain't no need to investigate our tax returns. Why are you really here?"

"Like I told you, sir, we're just trying to survey the tax returns." Kincaid said. Mary Washington glanced at her partner, hoping the older man would buy the story.

No such luck. "Son, if y'all really wanted to survey the tax returns, y'all would be callin' us in askin' us to bring our returns for seven or more years back. Now, I may be suspicious, but I don't think you're really from the IRS, are you?" Bodine let that hang in the air for a minute, and then said, "Son, you want more than just our tax returns." Bodine kept a hard stare on the pair.

Washington looked at her partner, and then sighed. "All right Mr. Bodine, you win. There is more to this. Did you serve in Vietnam?"

"Guess that had to come out." Bodine said calmly. "Who are you really? Those were some really fine fake ID's. . ."

"How did you know they were fakes?" asked Kincaid, astonished.

"You just told me." Bodine smiled, and then laughed. "I have been out of this town, and, I have seen a bit of the world. Yes, I was in Nam. The usual year hitch."

"Why haven't you told anyone?" asked Washington. "This would have been one hell of a story. . ."

"For the same reasons we didn't tell anyone about us in the first place." Bodine replied. "We liked the quiet." He relit his pipe and took a few puffs. "Young lady, I don't like the fact we have been found out. I like it even less, and you want to make me famous. I've earned my peace and quiet."

"Mr. Macabee, our magazine is willing to pay you for your story. Our cable network is willing to pay you for the rights to your story. You know, it might help if there was some way to tell people about what happened here. People get scared about what they don't know." Washington said.

"Can't you see that the fear mongers are out there, and they're about to take advantage of your very determined silence?" Kincaid added quickly. "Fear will fill the vacuum if no one will say what happened here. Your son, right now is being examined. If the doctors don't say what changed you, you have to."

"Don't you see that? You have to say something, or this town could be dead in the water if some fanatic decides to try and torch the place." Washington said. The pair fell silent, then she said; "Mr. Macabee, don't you think it should be you or someone like you that tells your story, and not some hack who won't even respect the truth as you know it?"

Bodine took three more puffs from his pipe and said, "Let me ask you for three days to make up my mind. That way, I'll know if I can sleep when I choose. Who do you work for?"

"Time Warner," Kincaid said, almost holding his breath. He looked at Washington who crossed her fingers.

"Three days. You can go now."

Kincaid would have turned a flip in midair if he didn't know that Bodine could still say no. He and Washington didn't let out their whoops until they were out of sight of the house.

Bodine went inside and called Time Warner to check if the two were legitimate.

Peter Devires, Jr. sat at the table in the kitchen. He wasn't married; it didn't matter since the hookers he went out with were the only girls that would look at him. He wasn't particularly ugly, it was just the hate seemed to be just under the surface most of the time, and he liked to get a black girl in his house, use her, beat her up and not pay her after he threw her out. That happened twice before the last girl he tried it on cut him nicely across the face and told her friends about it.

The hookers weren't even talking to him anymore.

He'd been the son of a Protestant minister who couldn't handle him and threw him out of the house when he heard his son planning to burn a cross on the front lawn of a black family. Peter Devires, senior told his son that he had no quarrel with these people. Junior shouted back that he'd been brainwashed by the bleeding hearts who wanted "them" marrying "our" kind.

That was ten years ago.

Peter Devires, Jr. sat at his kitchen table looking over his plans for the attack on Four Corners, drinking his favorite beer, and feeling mighty proud of himself. This would be bigger than a simple cross-burning, bigger than the unsolved murder of a Black, bigger than the running off a Mexican family by burning down their house and firing shots as they fled for their lives.

All Peter Devires, Jr. could think of was his hate. All he could think of was how everyone he came in contact with started our liking him, then when they found out his views and his temper, making sure they were well out of reach of him.

Damn that Darlene!

Taking his son from him and changing her name and getting away from so he couldn't follow her and take the boy back. . .

He'd get them all.

In the meantime, he had this.

The whole thing would be like a military maneuver (he'd get even with that dirty piece of trash nigger that got him kicked out of the marines. . .) Everyone would be in place to make the first strike on one of the city hall, just to serve notice their time was over, and they would not threaten to take over from real human beings.

Tomorrow was Tuesday.

Tomorrow would be the most glorious thing he'd ever do for true humanity.

Tomorrow, he would go down in the history books as a hero.

Tuesday dawned beautifully as Four Corners came to life. The farmers were out with their produce lined the stalls in the Farmer's Market. People went about their business as people do all over town. Children went to school and the parents took care of things.

All in all, it was a perfect Tuesday morning.

Six trucks came from all directions and headed for the city hall. Out came military rifles and machine guns spitting out steel jacketed death. Several bundles of high explosive flew toward shop windows and groups of people. Some recovered enough to grab their weapons and fire back at the fleeing trucks, and the sheriff and his men came at them, guns blazing. One of the truck's tires got hit and it rolled over, trapping the occupants inside. They were immediately arrested by more than irate citizens who didn't like that they had to hold them for the sheriff's deputies who roughly tossed them into jail with no regard for their injuries.

Two other trucks were caught in a crossfire that blew out tires and windows on the speeding vehicles. One tried to correct a skid that took it three hundred yards and into a telephone pole. Several people had automatic rifles trained on the hurt, bleeding occupants. One died because he was in the truck bed and lost his grip and was thrown into a brick wall head first.

The other tried to run a blockade of two big rigs that closed off the escape route. The driver was stupid enough to think he could get past them. The rigs were not moved and the truck and two of the occupants were decapitated. Two more were thrown from the truck when it rolled several times and slid into a grass field. The driver was the only one that survived, and he was placed in an ambulance that took him to a secured area in the town hospital.

The fourth, fifth and sixth trucks headed straight for the city hall with the sheriff and his deputies in hot pursuit, sirens screaming. The three trucks split off and the pursuit did the same. One went to a school yard and opened fire, hoping the followers would stop to help the injured. No such luck. The teachers waved to them to keep following and the accelerator went to the floor as the enraged pursuit sped up and turned down a side street and cut them off. The deputies jumped out of the car and raised their weapons and fired.

The truck was hit with a barrage that shredded the front of the truck and tore through the cabin hitting the skinheads in the truck bed. The truck wrapped itself around a telephone pole.

The deputies ran up to the truck and heard groans. One of the skinheads had been thrown from the vehicle. A deputy shot him, silencing him. The other groans stopped with the last breaths of the skinheads who were barely alive, stopped breathing.

The fifth truck headed for the town hall, but it was cut off by a carload of deputies that rammed the vehicle, sending it into a skid the driver tried to control, but lost it when he over corrected and it went into a 360 degree spin that ended with a blown tire flipping the truck over end and landing on its' roof. The truck was quickly surrounded and the skinheads who could crawl out were arrested. The others were taken away in body bags.

The sixth truck was driven by Peter Devires Jr. himself and he could drive. He too headed for the town hall and had his target in sight. He screamed for his men to lob the high explosives at the building. The explosions blew out the front of the building, injuring those who couldn't take cover in time. Most had heard the noise and moved as far away from the front of the building as quickly as possible. Some didn't quite make it.

Devires shouted with joy as he sped away from the scene with the sheriff in pursuit. Jim Mosley cursed as he followed, feeling that they should have expected this better than they did. Deep in his heart, he knew they'd done everything possible, which is all they could have done. "Frank, I want that son of a bitch cut off!"

"You got it sheriff!" Frank Jackson said. He cut across the park in the middle of the town square and got in front of the fleeing vehicle, forcing Devires to hit his brakes and turn sharply to avoid hitting the car. Another car with more deputies pulled up behind the truck, effectively trapping it. Devires tried getting out and running, but a shot from Mosley's gun that hit him in the leg causing him to fall to the ground in front of a bullet ridden car.

Mosley stood over the bleeding felon and pointed his gun at Devires head.

"Do it." Devires gasped staring with the kind of hate that might burn if Mosley cared.

An ambulance drove up. "He didn't die?" Mac Turner asked as he joined the sheriff.

"KILL ME YOU FREAK!" Devires shouted.

Mosley didn't even hear him. He put the handcuffs on Devires and helped Mac put him in the ambulance.

11. VICTIM? VICTIM?

Thursday morning.

Reverend Peter Devires, Senior walked in the Four Corners sheriff station and went to the counter. "Hello, I'm Peter Devires, Senior. I understand my son is being held here."

Jessica Davis stood up from her desk. "You're his father?"

Devires, Sr. nodded grimly. "Yes. I received his call last night." He looked at the remarkable young woman with the no nonsense demeanor. "I'm sorry about what happened. . ."

"It isn't your fault. He's responsible for his own actions. He chose to do what he did." Jessica said. "Bail hasn't been set yet, and the judge won't get here until two days from now."

"So that means that he won't be arraigned today?" asked Devires, Sr.

"That's correct." Jessica said. "I have to check with the sheriff before I let you in to see him."

"I understand he was shot in the leg."

Jessica held her first through fifth thoughts. "I know we're different, I know we're scary to some people. But he had no call or right to shoot up our town. If he gets out on bail, I can almost guarantee he won't live to see a trial. I'll admit to you, I wouldn't mind putting the bullet in him. I don't think any jury in the world would convict me or anybody else for doing it. Take a seat."

Devires, Sr. did so knowing that he had to do what he came to do and leave. He looked around him and he saw the stares of people who glanced at him, made some comment then looked away or went back to work. He'd signed in and some of them went to the register and saw his name.

One large four armed man glared at him, the double pupil eyes burning him to the quick. "You're a Devires, huh? Is the puke in custody your son?"

Devires, Sr. looked him in the eyes. "Yes, he is my son."

"Some piece of work; you saw the damage?"

"Yes I did."

"You proud of him?"

The double pupil eyes seemed to look into his soul. Devires, Sr. seemed to guess there wasn't any animosity directed at him. "Look, my wife and I have had this trouble with our son since he was a boy. We never taught him to hate. He chose to."

It was a long silence as the big man examined him. He could see the two armed man was scared, and standing over him wasn't helping any. "There are twenty dead, including six children in a schoolyard. I think you ought to tell him his body count. I feel sorry for you that the kid turned out the way he did, mister." The big man walked away.

Devires, Sr. sat there, not looking at any one until Jessica came for him. She introduced the man who came with her. "Reverend Devires, this is Sheriff Jim Mosley, who made the arrest. He'll take you to see your son."

"How did you know . . .?" Devires, Sr. asked.

"It's in his file. I called for it when he was arrested." Jessica said, and then went to her desk.

"Sheriff, if you could take me to my son?"

"Right this way, Reverend." Mosley led the way to the cells downstairs. "I have a question. How did your son turn out this way? We haven't done anything to him or anybody else."

"I'm afraid my son came on this himself. We never taught him to hate anybody else." Devires, Sr. said. "I admit I'm not all that happy about a lot of things that happened in the last few weeks."

"Anybody ever does anything to him when he was younger?" asked Mosley as they went down two levels. "See, I don't believe that he wasn't taught, so forgive me if I find it hard to believe he didn't learn it from you."

"My wife and I never taught him to hate. He came on that himself when he started hanging out with these skinheads. All I know is that he burned crosses on people's lawns, and I'm sure he's done things I don't know about. The last time I was at his house, he had a stockpile of weapons. He said it's for the coming race war when whites will have to struggle for supremacy of this country."

"Yeah, I saw a map once where all the races were supposed to get their own little portion of the country and stay there. Like it's gonna happen." Mosley said. They came to the cell where Peter Devires, Jr. lay on the cot with his back to the cell door. "Devires, you got a visitor."

Devires, Jr. turned and faced the two men. "Well, pop, I see the freaks dragged you out here."

"I came out here because I thought I might find out why you did this." His father said.

"Is the freak gonna stand there listening to us?" Devires, Jr. said.

"I'm just here to make sure you don't attack him." Mosley said. "I figure if you can shoot up a town, you could kill your father." He went to stand next to the wall opposite the cell.

"He's not the reason I'm here." Devires, Sr. said. Father and son stared at each other for a long time. "Why?"

"You know why."

"No I don't. What in heaven's name happened to you?" Devires said. "I raised you on the Bible. I tried to teach you right from wrong! Is what you did a Christian thing to do?"

"You mean I'm supposed to accept that-" he pointed at Mosley "-as being natural? Niggers have the right to marry whites? What else am I supposed to accept? They're going take over this country that normal white people built, that we tamed and took from savages that didn't know what to do with it! This country is for true human beings. That means whites, only. Nobody else has the right to be here except as our slaves. If they won't be slaves, they can be dead." He fell silent.

"I think you ought to know, until you attacked this town, no one here knew you were alive. You had no problems with us until you shot up the place." Mosley told him. "We would have been happy if nobody knew about us at all. Besides, you're the type that wants trouble, no matter how safe you are. You just can't leave people alone. You got five more minutes."

"That won't be necessary, Sheriff. He's still the same." Devires turned to leave. "Your mother and I can't stand with you over this. I can only hope you don't go free. You're safer in prison." He walked out the room, Mosley following.

Thursday afternoon.

It had been all over the television courtesy of all the reporters and news crews. Bodine Macabee had made his decision to talk after he'd talked with the mayor. Conners didn't like the idea, but he agreed they had to talk to the media and show them what the town was about. The silence was killing them.

Friday morning.

Mary Washington and Jeff Kincaid were at Bodine's house that morning with two reel to reel recorders and various and sundry video equipment and the people to handle it. It amused Bodine to see the eagerness in their faces as they realized they were getting the story of the year. Bodine wore his suit without the tie (he hated ties), and had polished his shoes even if they wouldn't be seen on camera. He'd also dragged out his photo albums with the pictures he'd taken at the time, along with the diaries he'd kept. They were a very complete record of his service in the army.

During the setting up for the interview, Bodine walked outside to get some fresh air. The truck had been parked away from the garden to make sure that none of the vegetable were crushed under its' wheels. He walked for some time and realized he'd gone to the road that led to his place and watched the cars roar past the turnoff. Somewhere along the way, he found his eyes full of tears for the loss of the privacy the town had come to value and cherish. He realized he liked that no one knew they were here. He wanted the silence back, the innocence of not having to deal with a cynical world that would see them as just another thing to be exploited then be discarded when the craze was over. He sighed, and then turned back for the house. . .

. . . And saw the camera truck with its camera aimed right at him following him as he made his way back. He looked at everything but them, kicking pebbles and rocks, picking up one or two and throwing them off to the side and generally giving them the perfect (although he didn't know it at the time) opening shot for the interview. The camera followed him until he went inside and said; "you ready?"

Friday morning.

The town was sweeping up. There had been no looting because the citizens were out in force to kill that idea. Grim faced, they watched all strangers who came to see the aftermath of the rampage. Some shots were fired at those foolish enough to try looting. Some looters were hit, but none were killed. Shopkeepers swept away the glass and debris while giving curt answers to the news people who asked their banal questions about how they felt and did they think this meant that any future relations with the outside world were damaged. The town bore it as best they could, all of them waited for Bodine's interview to come on to judge how they might be treated by the press. Tom Hannon and his daughter, Missy

Jean were tearing out the ruined window of their bakery, while next to them, George Taylor and his two sons, Rick and David were putting on the finishing touches of an all-night installation of a new window and door to their place. It was like this everywhere the rampage occurred.

The town met in the high school gym to discuss what they would do to pay for the damage. When a reporter asked if federal funds might be available he was ignored as the local banker promised low cost loans to help pay for the damage and the representative from the hospital pointed out that those who were injured would have extra time to pay for treatment. The town shocked the reporters by ignoring them and their suggestions that the government might be able to help.

Hattie McDaniel got up and stood proudly. "What you people don't seem to realize is that we have been taking care of our own for over forty years. If the government wants to help, fine. If they don't think the money should come here, fine. But as far as we're concerned, it really don't matter. We will get past this and on with our lives." She sat down to thunderous applause.

Mike Conners stood up. "I am glad that the alleged men who went on this rampage were stopped. I think we should give a great big hand of thanks to our sheriff, Jim Mosley." Mosley stood and accepted the applause. "Now," Conners continued, "I think we have to admit, we have no choice about what happens next. I think you all know that right now, Bodine Macabee is being interviewed. I think you also know that his boy, Cody, is being examined by the federal authorities. I don't like this any more than you do, but I really don't see any other way. I don't mind telling you, I am scared as to how this thing will go and how it will be received by the rest of the country. I'm going to ask you to hold your fire until it airs sometime next month."

The murmuring grew louder until Earl Monroe stood up and said; "Mike, you know the media ain't got no respect for nobody. They gonna tear poor Bodine apart." The crowd agreed with him.

Conners held up his hands. "I know, I know. But there's really no choice. We have to kill the speculation that is growing around us. I want y'all to do your best and try not to punch out too many of the reporters. . ." That got a lot of giggles and laughs that were devoid of humor. "In all seriousness, we can't go back to what we were. The world's here now, and we gotta go through this to get our peace of mind back. We won't be the same. I just hope you will do your best to get through this. Please?"

The gathered townspeople grimly nodded their assent, got up and went back to their now changed lives. Tomorrow was going to be hard.

12. DIALOGUES

Friday afternoon.

Cody Macabee sat in the almost comfortable room in a chair that faced four people and video recorders, microphones, and several stenographers.

Bodine Macabee sat in his living room with video cameras, microphones, and a pretty blonde woman who had a stack of questions from all over the country that had been solicited by CNN. Bodine had decided Time Warner would get the print.

Cody faced his questioners grim faced.

Bodine faced his calmly, even managing to smile. He looked good with a smile.

Both happened at the same time.

The room Cody sat in was electric with expectation. He knew about the men from Four Corners who served in the Vietnam War. The government came in sixty-eight wanting to know why so many conscious objectors came from here.

They found out.

They practically rubbed their hands with glee.

The army conscripted one hundred and fifty of the young men of age.

Those young men made terrifying soldiers.

It did not make a difference. The war was a lost cause.

President Nixon threw up his hands, shouted "WE WIN!" And then pulled out of Vietnam....

Of the one hundred fifty young men from Four Corners who went, one hundred and twenty can back in one piece. Of the thirty other, twenty came back with missing limbs; ten were killed in action including Cody's older brother, Barton.

Cody tried to keep the contempt off his face as the feeding frenzy began.

Bodine thought of Barton, too, and wondered if any of these people really gave a damn. So did Cody.

They both knew they did not matter. But they would if they had any say in the matter.

Let the inquisition begin.

Cody was first.

"I'd like to know who I'm talking to." Cody said.

"Fair enough, Mr. Macabee." The first one said. "I'm Harrison Bannister. To my right are Franklin Pace, Jennifer Honore and Benjamin Harris. What we want to do is find out how you happened."

"So you can prevent it from happening again?" Cody asked coolly. "How normal of you...."

"There's no need for that attitude, Mr. Macabee." Pace said. "We are not your enemies."

"Really..? I don't suppose you will also recommend that we be sterilized?" asked Cody. "I know who you are, Mr. Pace. I heard what you said the other day, and read your full statement in the paper. You are my enemy."

Pace reddened slightly, and then composed himself. "Mr. Macabee, I...."

"....Have no excuse for judging me before you met me. All we did was to conceal ourselves so we wouldn't have to face this." Cody was not backing down. "My family, my friends, my town is now the target of fear and/or exploitation. You are the real monsters."

Jennifer Honore spoke quickly. "Mr. Macabee, you must understand, we need to reassure the public they are in no danger. Surely you can understand that?"

"They have never been in any danger." Cody said firmly. "The danger will come when this interview is over." He paused glanced at the ground then back at his questioners. "After this is over, I'm going home to defend the town."

"From who..?" Honore asked.

"From the rest of the world, this planet's gonna be on us like dog shit on a shoe." replied Cody, as he looked at her.

Honore could not help but look at the double pupil eyes. She got up to look at them closely. Cody let her as he kept his arms folded on his lap. The others got up and did the same, marveling at the complexity of them. "How well can you see with those eyes?"

"I have excellent night vision...." Cody started.

"I'll bet." said Bannister.

"....and I have twenty-twenty vision up to three miles on a clear day." He finished.

"Anyone can see for three miles on a clear day." Pace said unimpressed.

"And read a page from a bestselling paperback book top to bottom?" Cody said.

"You're joking?!" Honore sputtered.

Cody shook his head no.

Bannister sat down. "How the hell did you happen? You're not even supposed to be born!"

Cody sighed. "Life is strange, we're here, get used to it."

Pace found his voice. "You told the doctors that it was possible that polluted water was the cause of your mutation. How do you know for sure?"

Cody spoke frankly. "We examined both the parents and children and found traces of the chemicals in their bodies. The ammiotic fluids in the mothers had significant levels, and so did the infants blood. We looked at the fathers' semen and the mothers' ovaries."

Honore asked, "Did the parents know what was happening to them?"

"No."

"What were the general reactions of the parents?" asked Bannister.

Cody took a deep breath. "Many people were understandably shocked. Some killed the infants out right, some abandoned them, and many people had themselves sterilized. The children who were abandoned were found by Lorraine Dozier, and many people left children on her door step."

The questioners watched as Cody stopped and took a deep breath. This was not easy for the four-armed man. Cody felt like an informant. The pit in his stomach grew tighter. He could see the mix of fear and fascination on their faces and no matter how they reassured him, Cody felt like they would forever treat him like the sample under the microscope. He looked at them and their steady gazes, knowing they considered him something to be controlled.

"I'm going to say this. All of you seem to have this idea that I'm something you own. I am not, and you do not." Cody said with his lower hands clenching and unclenching until his upper hands grabbed them. "Don't think I can't see it in your eyes that you think I'm some kind of monster you have to keep caged. Your fear makes you my enemy."

Jennifer Honore looked at her colleagues, and then said: "Mr. Macabee, we are not a lynch mob; we are not here to put a collar on you or cage you." She licked her lips, and then took a sip of water. "Please try to see it from our side. You and your friends happened and none knew about you. Our job is to see how you came to be, and report our findings."

Bannister jumped in. "May I call you Cody?"

"No."

Bannister recovered quickly. "You have to understand that the federal government has to be sure that this sort of thing is studied, and if possible, contained. We need to reassure the public that their water is safe, that the problem has been taken care of. That is fair. Mr. Macabee, we're all scared, and your cooperation will help."

Pace spoke. "That you and your people have managed to learn as much as you have is important to us and the country. It certainly showed courage, and initiative. We're hoping that you also have no ulterior motives with all you've learned. Your facilities are being inspected as we speak and a report to the president and congress will be made. Like it or not, any of us, we are in the same boat, and we must know who else in there with us. Surely you can see that?"

Cody could see that, and it bothered him. They made it sound perfectly reasonable, and that scared him. "Suppose the government does decide to take over? What then? Spaying and neutering?"

"Please. Don't even joke about that." Honore said. "We don't think it will come to that."

"But you can't be sure." Cody said. "There goes the fan."

Benjamin Harris spoke. "Mr. Macabee, do you know a Doctor Sam Murdock?"

"Town knows him."

"He was one of the doctors that did the investigation in the fifties?" asked Harris.

"Yes."

"He was one of the people, along with Lorraine Dozier, who began teaching the children how to hide their, for lack of a better word, mutation?"

"Yes."

"She showed how the children could hide themselves at a town meeting?" asked Honore.

"Yes." Cody said. "If you know all of this, why are you asking me?"

"We're just confirming the information we have." Pace interjected quickly. "We must be sure. . ."

"Look, people," Cody spat. "This is common knowledge in town. This is a useless pop quiz! Ask some real questions before I leave!"

Harris raised his hands before the protests really could begin. "He's right. All of this has been confirmed, and we really do need to move on. Jennifer?"

"Thank you, Ben." She said. "Mr. Macabee, when you realized you didn't look like the children on say, television, what did you do?"

"I asked my father why I was so different. He figured if I could ask, I should know. He told me. I didn't understand it at first, but I learned what went on before."

"You simply accepted it?" Honore asked.

"What else could I do?"

"You could have panicked." She replied.

"Not when I went to school the first day and saw so many children like me." Cody said. "There we were allowed to be without the restraints."

"Weren't there any two armed children there?" Honore asked. "Surely, there had to be two armed children. . ."

"There were none, until we went to regular school, then I met the first two armed child in my life."

"How did you feel?" asked Honore, "Did they find out?"

Cody smiled. "I felt sorry for them."

The four in front of him and their secretaries and camera operators stared at him. "You felt sorry for them?!"

Again, Cody smiled. "Yes. Even with the restraints, I thought I was special, and I had a secret they could never guess. My eyes were hidden under contact lenses, so they couldn't see those. Heh, I had learned to spot the kids with the extra arms by the way their bodies were shaped. After a while, the two armed kids figured something was up, and one of them managed to get a group of their friends together to hold me down and rip my shirt off, and then all hell broke loose."

"In what way . . .?" Pace asked.

"Well, the two armed kids parents figured, if they were lucky, their children would never know. By the time we were in high school, it was all but useless. Every two-armed kid in town knew about the four-armed kids."

"Didn't some of them reject you?" Pace asked again.

"Of course," Cody said. "When they grew up, they moved. But they kept their silence."

"Why do you think they stayed silent?" asked Harris.

"I have no idea; you'll have to ask them." Cody said. "But I think it had to do with some of them finding out they would or could have a four-armed baby. They left town very quickly so that no one else but them and their doctor would know."

"Did they keep their children?" asked Harris as he glanced at the others.

"Once they were home, they found they had a support system that would do all it could to make it less traumatic. It wasn't easy.'

"I dare say." Pace said quiet. The four realized why this was so important to them, more than just what had gone before. This was a town so tight knit they would have the hardest time going in cold and trying to get these answers. "Once your town established their situation, did you start looking for others that were affected outside of town?"

"We did pollution checks downriver, and some cases stumbled across someone who was four-armed. We then invited them to town."

"Did they need psychological help?" asked Bannister.

"In many cases, yes"

"How far did your investigations go?" asked Pace.

"We went as far as a hundred miles downstream and did tests. By then, the chemicals had filtered down enough so that any mutations would be rare."

"But you're not sure if there were no more mutations." Pace said. "Didn't you ask if any unusual births occurred?"

"Not as well as we should have. But no matter what you may think, we made the best effort we could at the time without revealing ourselves." Cody said.

"Did you find any others at the time?" asked Honore.

"We did, and in some cases, they children were given to us outright. The parents just couldn't cope." He paused, leaned back in his chair, then fixed his eyes on his questioners. "You don't know the shape some of them were in. I will not describe. The horror for many of these people were so great, they abandoned them. When these children found out who we were, they pleaded with us to take them with us. We did of course, and they have no wish to see their families again."

Cody went silent again remembering the first time he'd seen his first outsider mutant. The girl had sores on her back and legs, along with a severe case of VD. She had one child, and was pregnant with another. She could barely talk, and her little girl was almost as bad. They put the word out that there was a place "unique" people could go if they needed a place to stay. Some had come, but there would be a flood, now, Cody thought since the town was out in the open. He knew that someone who needed them would be coming to a new and healing home. That thought seemed to flare in his mind like a star. Tell the story. Let them know about Four Corners. They needed to know.

Cody continued.

At the same time, Bodine Macabee was having a different interview. Mary Washington and Jeff Kincaid were in his living room. Jeff had done the print interview; Mary would handle the television one.

"Hello and welcome to the quiet home of Bodine Macabee. I'm Mary Washington, and this is INSIDE AMERICA JOURNAL." Mary waited for the count that told her they would slug in the opening of the show. "Hello again, tonight, my guest is Bodine Macabee, the father of Cody Macabee, the four-armed young man who is being examined by the government. Ever since the town of Four Corners became known to the world, everyone has wondered how such a thing as multiple armed people could happen. Bodine Macabee has lived here his entire life. He too is four armed, but chooses not to show his extra arms." She turned to Bodine. "Good evening, Bodine."

"Good evening, Mary." Bodine replied.

"I understand you were one of the first white children who were raised by Lorraine Dozier?"

"Well," Bodine started in his drawl, "My parents couldn't take that they'd had a four-armed baby. So they abandoned me on Mama Dozier's doorstep."

"So you grew up with her as a mother?" asked Washington.

"She was the only mother I knew since my parents didn't want to know about me."

"I see. Didn't this make you feel abandoned?" She asked.

Bodine shrugged. "It didn't matter, since I had a mother in Mama Dozier." He shrugged again. "Even with all the children, she made us all feel loved, and we knew no different."

Mary smiled, and pointed to the albums on the table in front of them. "You have some pictures of Cody as a child. . ." She picked up the top one, the one Bodine knew she wanted. "Here are some pictures of Cody in childhood. I notice there very few of you as a child."

Bodine smiled sadly. "With the expense of taking care of all of us, Mama didn't have the money to have pictures taken on a whim. We took pictures once a year, after we hustled bottles for the money."

"It must have taken you a long time." Mary said.

"Not that long. Of course, we did take a well-deserved candy break now and then." said Bodine. Mary and the watching crew laughed as Bodine found a picture. "That is me, about ten years old." He pointed to another. "I'm about seventeen here."

"Didn't you find it difficult being different as you are?" asked Mary. "I mean, the pressure on you to keep the secret must have been enormous."

"It was, since you couldn't be out in the open. In a way, this is all a relief." He found another picture. They would show up on screen later as insert shots.

"These are friends of mine at Mama's. Every last one of them has children, now, and I think the kids were getting antsy to let the arms out, and to hell with what other people thought. I think we would have been found out eventually. Everything is found out, eventually."

"When you started on the road to knowing what changed you, did you ever think that the town would change so much?"

"Town had to, since the babies were born." Bodine said. "You have to realize that we'd been through a great big old trauma, and we had to know why. First, we started to learn about the body, and then when we sent our first students to college, the idea was for them to learn all they could, then bring it back to us. We began to teach it to the next and the next. The next step was to build a laboratory, everything. We had to know. No matter what, we had to know."

Mary looked at the shots of the first laboratory. "When you realized what happened, did any of you ask your children not to have children?"

Bodine shook his head no. "We couldn't tell them that. They had to decide that for themselves. They had children."

"Some might consider that selfish, after everything you'd been through."

"Maybe, maybe not; it's only natural you want children, and we wanted children. Now, it's way out of our hands."

"What do you mean by that?" Mary asked cocking her head.

"Well, now that we're known, we now have to cope with each other."

"Do you think it's possible?"

"I pray it is." Bodine said. "There's no way we're leaving without a fight."

"Are you looking for a fight?" asked Mary.

"Lord, no!" Bodine replied. "We just want to live as peaceably as possible. One of the things I have never understood is why people think those who are different are a threat. When you get right down to it, most of us don't care that you're alive."

"Do you think that signals a general indifference on your part?"

"I don't think so. What I mean is, I don't think we care until we know you're there, and after that, it's are you friend or foe? Some people have decided we're foes. Those are the ones I have no problem taking out like garbage."

"You mean like Reverend Jimmy Robertson?"

"There ain't nothing to revere about him. He's like that idiot, Devires, throwing punches before he's been attacked; stupid, both of 'em." Bodine's disgust was all over his face, and the cameraman made sure he got the shot. "Both of 'em are cowards."

"Some think they're heroes." Washington said.

"Then we're really messed up as a country, aren't we?" said Bodine, not taking the bait.

"I've seen the schools here. This place really stresses the basics, plus a heavy dose of the sciences. This town's schools are among the highest ranking in terms of academic performance in the world. . ." Mary began.

"Thank you."

"....I would have thought that would have brought people in here to see what was going on since is it agreed there is a general decline in education in this country's schools. Do you think that your town would be a model for the nation?"

"I don't know about that."

"What do you mean?"

"Well, first off, there are a lot of people out there that don't care about their kid's schools. First thing, you got to get the parents in there. Second, you got to allow the local districts to have a major say about what's needed. We did it without federal money. . ."

"But you had to do it without federal money."

"Exactly; it was mostly setting a standard, then sticking to it. Even in the sixties when they were changing everything, we decided to keep things as there were, then only change it when it wasn't relevant anymore."

"So that means, as the knowledge changed, you changed what you taught."

"Exactly; See people forget that learning is a skill, and most schools don't teach how to learn. They also don't praise, and most importantly, this country really doesn't value learning, period. We call people who want to learn all sorts of names, we make fun of those who are more inclined to think first rather than just go with their emotions. Emotions are important, but they aren't the only thing that matter."

"Are you saying we should grow up?"

"That would help. I don't meant become robots, I just mean try to find out what's going on first, then get upset if it warrants it. You can't just fly off the handle because someone tells you your child is misbehaving. You have to realize you live with other people, and no matter how much you think the system is against you, it's also against everybody else."

"What do you think the solution is?" asked Mary. She was surprised as anyone in the room that Bodine was this articulate when he needed to be, and a deeper thinker than they thought.

"There is no one solution. Just change what you can, and deal with the rest. Trust in your God and yourself, and then trust the ones you trust. If they betray you, don't trust them or drop them. It'll be on their heads." Bodine said. "This town had to trust itself, and do what it could. If that is not enough for the rest of the country, well too damn bad. I think we were right."

Mary Washington shook her head in amazement. "You have been a surprising interview, Bodine, Thank you."

"You're welcome. I didn't mean to go on like that, you just got me started."

"I wish most of my interviews would get started like that, Bodine. Again, thank you. This is Mary Washington, good night for INSIDE AMERICA JOURNAL."

13. MAMA SALVATION

1947

Irene Lorraine Dozier picked up the newborn that had been deposited on her doorstep. The infant girl's cries nearly broke her heart. "Mama got you here now, child." She wrapped the baby in the blanket and brought it inside.

As she entered the front room of the four-room house, there were four beds, one in each corner. The eight children who slept in them played in the middle of the room. "Willie, get the toys you ain't using in the toy box before I slip on them, you hear?"

"Yes, Mama Dozier," Wille was a normal two-armed boy, ten years old who looked up and saw the bundle in her arms. "Another baby?"

"Fourth one this week; I don't know how long I can keep takin' them in." Mama Dozier said. Moving through the room, she entered a room with three other children in cribs. She put the newest arrival in an empty crib and pulled a blanket over the child. She checked on the other sleeping infants, then went to her garden and pulled fresh collard greens and okra into her apron, then went into the kitchen. She set about making dinner, and then came a knock.

"Mama Dozier?" a woman's voice called.

Mama Dozier looked out the window. "Jolene? Come on in."

"You about to make dinner?" Jolene asked as Mama Dozier put the remnants of a hambone into the pot of water.

Mama Dozier rinsed the collards well, then, as the water boiled, put them in. "Got to, girl. I got mouths to feed."

"I don't see how you could take them in." Jolene said. "My mama said the people who had those babies sinned terrible for them to be born that way."

"She did, huh?" Mama said. She started a pot of water, throwing two cups of rice when it came to first boil. She covered the pot when it came to second boil, covered it, turning the heat down to simmer. "How does she know it was sin?"

"Well, look at them." Jolene stammered.

Mama Dozier gave her a look, then said; "you sure you can tell by looking? That's what white folks say about us."

"Mama, all I mean is that, it ain't natural for people to be born like that." Jolene said. "Where they gonna live? How they gonna live? You ain't thought about that, have you?"

"As far as I can tell, neither have you." Mama Dozier said. "I guess I'm gonna have to figure out something, I don't know what, but I'll find it." Jolene started to say something, but Mama Dozier interrupted first. "I have no idea how, but there's got to be a way. These children just can't be allowed to die. Now If you don't want to see them, don't be coming around here talkin' no mess around me." She paused, and then continued. "I understand how everybody feels, but we just can't let them die, not like some of us want them to. As long as I got breath in my body, I will not treat them in any way evil. I don't know what caused it, but I know it ain't the sin of the parents. You can tell your mama that." A third pot was put on the stove with milk, then oatmeal. She made it thin so it could be taken from a bottle, and then filled the bottles for the infants feeding. She checked the greens again, along with the roasting sweet potatoes and cornbread in the oven.

Going into the other room, she gathered the children up and made them wash their hands and faces, then sit down at the long table outside the service porch. "And don't be getting in the dirt before the food gets out here." she warned.

"Let me tell you something else, Jolene," Mama Dozier said as she came back in. You might be havin' a baby pretty soon. I hope, for you I mean, it ain't like these children. It seems to be happening to everybody on our side of the tracks. If that's true, I'm gonna pray it don't happen to you. You just about the right age for it to happen to you."

Jolene went pale under her caramel skin. "It ain't gonna happen to me!" Her defiance wasn't convincing, and she knew it.

The next day, Mama Dozier went around to people who'd recently had children with a list of questions she'd worked up. She knew about the children who died, and she wanted to talk to the people who'd kept theirs.

Soon everyone on the black side of town knew what she was asking, and some came to her, knowing she was trying to figure out what happened. Soon, she had several thick three ring binders filled with all she found out. She came to believe that it was something everyone had in common. On a hunch, she started to boil, then distill the water she used with a homemade still. It scared her that it might be the water, and she'd notice a strange residue in the boiler that she had to scrape out. She saved some of it in a paper lined cloth bag.

Mama Dozier didn't realize it, but she'd hit on the solution thirteen ten years before the town would.

1960

Sam Murdock sat in the office of the converted warehouse that had been transformed into housing units where many four armed people and their families lived. It had started small when Mama Dozier first moved in, remaining cold and drafty for a long time. But now, it was a warm place with an enclosed play area for the children that romped with their arms out in the open. They were happy, and Murdock didn't begrudge them that. He was still staring at the children when Mama Dozier came in. She joined him at the window.

"Been a long time comin', this place." Mama Dozier said. "But, at least it's finally here. You must be Doctor Murdock."

"Yes, I am." Murdock said. "I came to see you because of what I've learned about you. You took in abandoned babies around forty-five. . . "

"I had to. I couldn't let them die." Mama Dozier said.

"I also understand you asked around and got the parents to kick in for their care." Murdock said.

"As long as I didn't tell the children who the parents were, I got the money." Mama Dozier said sadly. "I used it to buy this place, beds, lots of blankets, school books and hire some help."

"I understand later on, the parents kicked in a little more so the place could be made livable." Murdock said. "You did a nice job."

"Thank you, Mister Murdock." Mama Dozier said.

"Uhm, Doctor Murdock."

"That's right, you called about the notes I made. Why do you want to see them? I thought you had it figured out." Mama Dozier asked. "All I could think of was that it had to be something we were doing."

"How far did you get?" asked Murdock.

"Well, I made lists of who'd given birth to a four armed child. I found out where they were born in our part of town. I did that around forty-seven. Turned out a year earlier, a baby had been killed by its' mother. I went to the grave and dug it up. It was four armed."

Murdock stroked his chin. "Lord..!" He fanned himself absentmindedly with his hat. "May I see your notes?"

"They're in my storage room." Mama Dozier said. "You come with me and we'll get them. Did you look at the water supply before they put in the water lines for the rest of the town?"

"We found traces of chemicals that might have had a hand in the mutations, but they were very weak."

"After a while, I figured it had to be the water, but I couldn't prove it. I distilled our drinking water just in case." Mama Dozier said.

"I hope you don't take this wrong. How far did you get in school?" asked Murdock.

"I got as far as twelfth grade. But I had to quit before I graduated because I had to go to work to support my family, then I got married. After we got this place started, I went ahead and started going back to school. I had to. I finally got my diploma last year, but I'd kept studying so I could take better care of the children. As they started to grow up, I made sure they went to school and studied hard so they could take care of themselves."

Murdock stared at her, not knowing what to say. This woman had figured it out. He stared at her with greater respect. He watched as she pulled out the double bag of boiled residue and set it on a nearby table. "That's the residue from the boiler, and," she squatted down to pull the notebooks from the pile she worked on, "here are the notebooks." She gave a grunt as she stood up. "These bones, gettin' old. . ." Standing, she asked, "How long you have been looking for this?"

"Ever since the children started coming on our side of the tracks; we started to realize this might be happening to you only recently."

"I guess y'all really do think the world turns around you." Mama Dozier said. "But, that ain't nothin' new."

"I guess we deserve that." Murdock said. "Especially now that we're all in the same boat, now…."

"What makes you think we ain't been in it?" Mama Dozier said as she opened up the top notebook. "This is the names of all the people who had the babies, and the year they babies were born." She turned the pages. "Most of them ended up with me, and I made sure the parents paid something to me to take care of them."

"Why?" asked Murdock.

The look she gave him told him he was a fool to ask. "They were helpless. As far as I was concerned, if they were alive when they came out, God meant for them to live." She told him with an iciness that scared him. "Are you sure you're looking for the why of these babies? If you ain't, nothin' will stop me from hunting you down."

"I'm sure I want to find out why this happened." Murdock said, taken aback this woman meant what she said. "Look, this is something that shouldn't have occurred. These children will be adults very soon, and we have to find some way of helping them cope with what makes them different. I'm surprised that you and the others I've talked to went to all this trouble."

"You didn't think we we're smart enough?" Mama Dozier said, the frost not gone from her voice. "Seems to me, you white folks have always taking us cheap. We ain't stupid. Remember that." She picked up the bag of residue and two of the books. "Well, get 'em! I ain't carrying them all by myself!" Chagrined, Murdock picked up the other notebooks and followed Mama Dozier out.

Back in her office, Mama Dozier put the notebooks on her desk and sat in her chair. "You can make copies of them, but I want them back."

"That's no problem. I want you to know these will help. I got a feeling we're going to be working together with these children." Murdock looked up at her. "Do you have notes on how they're growing up?"

Mama Dozier got up and went to her file cabinet and tapped it on the top. "All in here. I noticed how they would start crawling using the lower arms, and carry something in their upper arms. My late husband had a movie camera, and I filmed them crawling around like that. Henry developed the film himself since he was afraid to give it to anyone to develop. I'll have to go back up and get the film." She shook her head. "Strangest thing I ever saw. But whatever they started something new; I filmed it, just to have a record of it. I never thought you white folks would be interested in us with this problem, then I got Chester."

"Chester?"

"The first white baby left at my doorstep. Somebody saw a man stop his car and leave him. I found out who owned the car and tracked him down. They told me I was crazy, and then I came back with the baby." She looked at Murdock. "They didn't want pay nothin' at first, but I got 'em to when I told them that I would tell everybody they abandoned their baby on my doorstep. They paid."

"I'll bet!" Murdock grinned, and then he turned sober. "You have to understand, I never expected you have these kinds of records, for them to be as complete as they are, I ... I...."

Mama Dozier nodded her head. "I know." She found Chester's file. "Here it is."

"Chester's file...?"

"Uh-huh. I suggest you don't go after the parents. That's part of what keeps this place going, nobody knows who the parents are."

"The money's tight?"

"Always...."

Murdock looked at her. It occurred to him that he and a whole lot of other people underestimated the coloreds. It scared him how much he was coming to respect her. Not in the sort of condescending way he'd always done, it was different.

It was real respect.

"How can I help?"

It was Mama Dozier's turn to look at him strangely. "What are you talking about?"

"I'm talking about what can I do to help you with these children?" Murdock said. "They need schooling to be more than just 'good with their hands'. They need to be able to answer their own questions about what happened to them in the womb. That's going to come up, and they need to be taught how to move out in the rest of the world. It has to start now."

Mama Dozier stared at the white man in front of her, her mouth dropping open. "You are serious!?"

"Yes." Murdock said. "We can't afford to pull this colored/white nonsense with these children. There are more of them born every day. We can't keep hiding them."

"I have been thinking about that. I've begun to teach them how to read and write. I don't know how this is going to sound to you, but I've been trying to think of how to teach them science, among other things. . ."

"Such as…?" Murdock asked as he leaned forward.

"Well, making clothes, obviously. How to keep their eyes away from strangers. . ."

"That last may not be possible, and I see what you're getting at." He leaned back in his chair. "They have to be schooled. Mama Dozier, we need to talk to the town council and the schoolteachers. We've been approaching this from different ends. We need to make this a group effort."

"You think we can do it?" asked Mama Dozier. "People may not be ready."

"Well, ready or not, we've got to clean the fan. This town has to face up to what is ahead, like it or not. These are our children, and we can't keep hiding them. Colored or white doesn't matter anymore, we're in the same boat. You're the first to see that, and I need you to show the rest of the town. Will you help me?"

"I got to. The children are at stake." Mama Dozier said. "Let's get to work."

The council room was crowded.

It should have been, considering how fast the news had spread that Doctor Sam Murdock and Mama Lorraine Dozier were now working together.

The Mayor and the council members sat at the long straight oak table with Murdock and Mama Dozier to their right. As the council room filled up, some stared at her as they took their seats.

"Doesn't their staring bother you?" asked Murdock.

"Not as much as some of them hope." Mama Dozier replied. "Even with what we've got to say, they gonna be cursing me soon enough for being allowed to sit up here in the first place."

Jake Masters noticed how Murdock and Mama Dozier were talking between themselves softly. "What's that nigger doing up there?"

"They looking all kind of friendly, ain't they?" Mercy Jean Hammond said.

"You know who she is, don't you?" asked Lonny Vincent. "That's Mama Dozier."

Mercy Jean's mouth dropped open. "You mean that woman who took in all those children?!"

"Yeah," Lonny said. "I heard she gets money from the parents as long as she don't tell the children who their parents are."

"Damn!" Jake said. "That's right! She's also trying to get them some schoolin' while she's at it. I heard tell she's talkin' to the principal about gettin' some teachers over to the warehouse. And she's teachin' some herself."

"No wonder!" Mercy Jean said as she sat down. "I heard the four armed babies were born on the niggers' side of town first."

Lonny turned to her. "Where'd you hear that?"

"I heard Mrs. Thompson's man Jericho Walk talking to Mr. Putnam's man Franklin Hope how she took in the babies that were left on her doorstep. Then she went lookin' for the parents, found 'em, and that's how she got them to pay for her taking care of them."

"I heard some whites left their babies with her, too." Jake said. "Maybe she and the doc are working together?"

Mercy Jean gave him an odd look. "Why would he do that?"

"Maybe she figured somethin' he didn't?" said Lonny. The three of them gave each other puzzled looks.

The mayor gaveled the meeting to order. "Ladies and gentlemen, I wanna get this started. As you know, we have been giving birth to children with multiple limbs. What you don't know is that the coloreds have been birthing them first." The crowd murmured loudly, some people shifting in their seats. This woman knows, not just by accident or luck, how it all happened. . "

Jake Masters jumped from his seat. "Are you saying this nigger knew before we did what changed our children?!"

Sam Murdock spoke up. "I am saying she figured it was the water, and the food we grew using that water, changed us. Mrs. Dozier took sample of the water, boiled it, and got a chemical residue that she saved, since she didn't know who to trust to keep quiet about it."

Jake wouldn't sit down. "I cannot believe she figured out what was going on before we did! She's lying!" It was too much, and charged the stage.

Mama Dozier stood up, furious. "I am not a nigger, Mister!" Right then she didn't care if they lynched her or not. She only knew she had to defend herself without striking the enraged white man.

Sam Murdock stood up and blocked Jake's way. "You're gonna listen!" he hissed, "Because you can learn from her!" Jake glared at him, then her.

"There ain't nothin' no nigger can tell me....!" Jake hissed.

"Then I'm gonna tell. Those children are at school age. They need an education that will teach them how to deal with the world. Some of them are at puberty, now. 'That Nigger' has been doing more for them and this town than you have, Jake, and I think it's about time we made sure they are able to take care of themselves. We're gonna do it with or without you. Now why don't you sit down?"

The Mayor gaveled for attention. "What we have here is a colored woman who has begun what we need to do. Mama Dozier, would you pass out the book you and the doctor made?"

Mama Dozier got up, went to a table in front of the dais, picked up a stack of thick books, went to the first row, saying: "Take one and pass the rest along, please. Thank you." She passed out the rest, and then sat back down, glancing over at the doctor, who smiled. "Don't worry, the plan will work."

"I know it will, but will they believe me?" she asked.

"They'd better, knowing the children will rebel if we try to keep them hidden forever." Murdock looked over at the mayor, who nodded his head. Standing up, he began. "I'll get to the point. Many of you were here five years ago when we began to research why we were having four armed children. Mama Dozier has found a major clue as to why. It was the water from the river everybody drank from. Somehow, the chemicals in the waste water combined to affect our bodies. The children were supposed to be twins, but the split never fully happened."

One woman in the back of the room sputtered, "We poisoned our bodies and condemned our children to being freaks!" She collapsed in sobs.

"It can be condemnation, or we can do something about it." Mama Dozier said. The room turned to her. The pain was evident in their eyes. "These children, our children must be taught to fend for themselves. We must bring them out in the open, and teach them how to hide there."

"How do we do that?" Mercy Jean asked.

"I'd like to show you." Mama Dozier said as she waved to four young people in the back of the room, two black, two white. They came to the front, removed their over coats, then their shirts to reveal elastic wrappings of some kind. The girls wore training bras, the boys, in undershirts. Using their top arms, they opened the elastic wrap snaps as the mouths of the rest of the adults dropped open.

Mama Dozier looked on with approval. "I think we found a way for them to come out in the open." The room murmured with approval.

"You mean they gonna have to wear those straps to come out?" Jake asked. "Don't it hurt?"

"Not as much as not being able to go out." Chester, the white boy said. "I got tired of just being allowed to go out in the yard at home. I wanna see the rest of the town."

"Me, too." said Richard, the black youth. "We can't stay hid any more. Pretty soon, we're gonna be adults, then what do you do about it?"

The assembled adults looked at them and could see the truth in their eyes; with or without them, period.

"Oh, yeah," Chester said. "This nonsense about separate but equal has to go. We don't have the time for it. It's everybody or nobody."

"Wait a minute, boy!" Jake Masters jumped from his seat. "That is to protect you from the coloreds!"

Chester went to the man and grabbed him by the collar. "We don't have the time or the money to be playing 'I'm scared of the coloreds'. Nobody does. Me and Richard have plans to set up a small laboratory together. The girls will be working together. If you try to get in the way with this stupid bigotry of yours, then I say, we're better off with you dead." He let him go and walked back to his friends.

Stunned, Jake sputtered, "They ain't your kind. . ."

Chester's disgust was too apparent. "Wrong. You ain't my kind. I ain't been your kind ever since you left me on Mama's doorstep, daddy."

Jake stared in amazement at Mama Dozier. "You told him!"

"I didn't tell nothin'...." Mama Dozier went to Chester. "How did you find out? I didn't tell you!"

Chester looked at her, knowing his next words would get him grounded for a month at least. "After Doc Murdock came to the house, I wondered if he was my daddy. After you and he left for his office, me and Richard went in your files. We found our names, and the names of our parents. We knew if we were at the house, they didn't want us, but I had to know who my parents were." He held up his hands, staring at them. "I knew why they didn't want me, I didn't care about that. I just wanted to see them." He looked over at the horrified Jake. "What I saw made me sick. I saw a stupid, cowardly bigot who was afraid of coloreds, and I couldn't understand it. I saw how he treated that one colored man like garbage, and I was grateful he didn't raise me. I realized he was afraid of me, too. Don't you come near me, Jake Masters; I want nothing to do with you." He put the wrap back on, and the other children did the same.

"Y'all got to understand something. We have been without you for long, long time. We gonna find our answers." Richard said. "You ready Chester? Girls..?" The four of them dressed and left.

It was a long time before someone spoke. "My Lord, they seem older than us. . ."

Mama Dozier nodded her head. "I think it's because they have more of everything, they can think faster, take in lessons better, and they remember more. Those four..? I have to do college type lessons, and it's pushing me to the limit."

Everyone looked at everyone else. The kids were ahead of them. Way ahead of them. If they didn't act now, they would be left behind.

Jake, still white as a sheet, asked; "What do we do, now?"

Sam Murdock saw all the eyes were on him and Mama Dozier. "I think I have an idea. Are you with me and Mama Dozier?"

The room chorused "yes".

"Good. This is what we do. . . "

14. CREATING THE ENVELOPE

1962

Chester and Richard stood outside the small building that had become their laboratory. It was a converted four room shotgun house built in the nineteen twenties.

"I guess we gonna start now." Richard said. "We just about drove everybody crazy getting this house."

"You right about that." Chester replied. They did not hide their arms since they were in an isolated part of town. "I got a question. Did you understand that part about the way the DNA might have been affected by the chemicals in the water?"

"You unclear on something?" asked Richard.

"Well, I always did have a problem on how long it may have taken the chemicals to affect our parents. I'm assuming that since it took years, it might have been occurring as our parents were growing up, but didn't manifest until they started to have children."

"I think Doc Murdock thinks the same thing, and I agree with him. Now all we have to do is prove it." Richard said. "Another thing; we should find out if any towns down river are affected; if so, how."

"Doc said he took samples of the river water, and soils around the river. I wonder if he took any in further inland. After all, we did have that flood, what, four years ago?" Chester said. "If the river flooded before we were born with the chemicals in it, then it would have left them further out."

Richard nodded his head. "You're right. There's one problem. The chemicals content of the river water has been dropping since the plants around town closed. We should see if they have some residue, then compare it with the distilled stuff that Mama has." He looked at the ground. "You know, this has been pretty hard on everybody. You finally talk to Jake?"

"No. I need him like I need a hole in my head. I wanna keep my distance." Chester said. "I did go to see my mother. She's in bad shape. Doesn't want to see or hear anything. I even went two armed. She talks about her baby dying in childbirth, but she'll get over it."

"I'm sorry." Richard said.

"Not your fault. I guess that why I said the separate but equal crap had to go. I don't wanna lose my family. I need you, Rich." Chester said.

"I know what you mean, brother." Richard said, putting an arm around him, "I know what you mean."

Inside, most of the equipment was second hand and repaired. They scavenged from medical labs and high schools and colleges. By nineteen sixty-eight, the place had expanded to twenty acres, an electric fence, and armed security guards.

The oldest four armed children were now young adults who were going to college and having children. Like their parents, the children were taught to hide their differences and to keep cordial but discreet friendships. They went out into the world and studied at every college and university they could get into, then bringing their degrees and knowledge back to Four Corners. They did everything, branching out to environmental and chemical disaster concerns.

They got a reputation for handling the worst messes man could cause, and earned their fees by being the best.

They also got good at hiding themselves. Better restraints for their second set of arms plus contact lenses made it easy to move about in outside society. A strict set of rules for dealing with other people so there would be few if any births from outside of the town gene pool were created to keep the secret as long as possible.

There were of course, lapses. Those men and women who could deal with what they had found out became accepted into families. Those that couldn't, kept their mouths shut for fear of being made fools of, or at the very least, put away for insanity.

In the town, it was safe. There were areas where one could remove the wraps and stretch and run as free as a bird. These were carefully guarded, and no outsiders would know about them.

The schools were improved as well. The teachers got better because the parents and students demanded it. Incompetence was not tolerated in the least. The standards were set higher than any school, and they were met.

All this to puzzle out the why and how of the mutations.

1968

"There's a town called Four Corners in Georgia that has a lot of conscientious objectors to the draft." Major Raymond Beale said to his assistant, Corporal Eugene Kiley. "My assignment is to find out why."

"Perhaps they're very religious, sir?" said the corporal.

"Perhaps, I don't know. It might be the whole town objects to the war. Lord knows, it seems like everybody else does. You will accompany me, corporal."

"Yes sir." Kiley replied. "Sir, do you think this may be some kind of ruse?"

"It may be. But let's not speculate, corporal. Evidence, then decide."

"Of course sir," Kiley said. "What time do we leave, sir?"

"0600 sharp," Beale said.

The next afternoon the two men arrived in Four Corners in a plain sedan. Small town screamed at them from everywhere they looked.

"Nice place, sir." Kiley said, "Reminds me of home."

"Yeah, perfect little place." Beale said. "Real perfect," He took in his surroundings, then looked at his corporal. "Maybe too perfect…."

Kiley had gotten used to his superior's hunches. "Think there's something wrong, sir?"

"Could be; I know it's the afternoon, but let's get a motel room." said Beale. "Then I want to call on the local officials. Start with the mayor."

"Yes, sir," Kiley said.

Once the room was gotten and was done the pair made their way to City Hall.

"Gentlemen, I understand your curiosity, but I have ask, why not question the draftees directly?" asked Mayor Jim Harper after the introductions were made.

"It seems Mr. Mayor. . ." Beale began.

"Jim, please." Harper said.

"Well, Jim. It seemed a good idea to start with you, since your own son was a CO." Beale said.

Harper smiled a most convincing warm smile. "You must understand, Major that most of us here object to this war because we believe our country should not have gone into it. We don't believe we really have a direction there."

Beale arched an eyebrow. "And your sons agree?"

"Whole hearted, frankly, you will find the majority are against it." Harper said. "I'm sure you'll investigate and find I was right."

"I'm sure." Beale said, getting up. "Thank you for your time, Mr. Mayor."

"You're welcome." Harper said. He got the door for them.

Once outside, Beale said, "He's hiding something big."

"Do you want me to look around?" asked Kiley.

Beale rubbed his chin. "We'll both look, try to make it look like we're checking out the town. You go to the local recruiter's office. Find out what you can there."

"Yes, sir," Kiley said. "I don't know about you sir, but I've noticed most everyone averts their eyes to us."

A young man passed the two of them by. His eyes darted away from them. "I see what you mean. . . "Beale said. "Let me try something. . ." He approached a young man wearing dark glasses. "Excuse me, could you tell me why people look away from us when we glance at them?"

The young man looked them both over; "The army here in this town?" He took a step away from them. "Look, mister, I'm CO., okay? Most of my friends are the same. Last thing we need is John Wayne telling us we got to die in some strange country. That ain't right. I ain't crazy 'bout you either." He backed away, turned, and then ran.

"Damn. . ." Beale looked over at Kiley. They both stared after the retreating form. "Let's go. . ."

"Where?" asked Kiley.

"Recruiting office," said Beale. "Double-time."

At the same time, Jim Harper was on the phone to Jake Masters. Jim knew Chester, Jake's son never spoke to his father after the meeting with Sam Murdock and Mama Dozier.

It hurt the man more than he could say.

Jim had to try and get the man and son to reconcile since the army was now in town to find out why so many were conscientious objectors. He'd already called everyone else. This could be a disaster. The phone rang ten times before Jake picked it up.

"Who is this?" Asked Jake in his rasp, gotten from one too many cigarettes he refused to give up.

"It's me, Jake." Jim said knowing the tone in Jake's voice said he didn't want to talk to anyone. Tough, Jim thought. "I need to talk to you."

"Well, you got me on phone, what is it?" growled Jake.

"There are some men from the army in town, and they want to know why no one from this town is going to the armed forces. They may find out about the kids. . ."

"What the hell do I care?! Let 'em find out we been birthin' freaks! Might just come in and clean the town of 'em. . ."

Harper listened to Jake's speech closely.

It was badly slurred. Harper shook his head; drunk again. "Look, if they find out. . ."

"They fuckin' find out! Let 'em." Jake shouted, slamming the phone down.

Harper made one more call. It was picked up on the third ring.

"Hello?"

"Chester? It's Jim Harper. Listen, there were two men from the army wanting to know why no one from town was going into the army." Harper said. "I told 'em what I think you'll tell them, but they will look around."

"I heard." Chester told him. "Marty Ryan told me on my way home from the lab. My old man knows?"

"I just called him. He sounded drunk; chewed my head off, too. I don't think he'll say anything, but. . . "Harper said.

"I'm not gonna talk to him, he won't listen to me. Jim, no matter what happens; we gotta keep this town together on this. I can't help but feel something is gonna happen." Chester said. "I think Jake's the least of our worries."

"I agree. Somehow we've got to convince them they don't need us." Harper said slowly. "That won't be easy."

"I know. Let's face it; we don't have much of a choice." Chester told him. "We don't want what's happened here to get out."

"What if it does?" asked Harper, his voice tight.

"Let's hope we never get to that bridge." said Chester.

Now

Chester watched his grandchildren playing in the large front yard of his son's house. Bobby was watering the flower garden and keeping an eye on his four. Jessie Mae just drove up and her three fell over each other getting out of the back of the minivan as Carl turned off the engine and put it into park. All of them four armed, all of them Chester's family. Chester got up and went to the kitchen window and said, "Jessie Mae and Carl are here, along with of the four horsemen."

"Chester, stop that!" Kathy, his wife said. "You know you're glad to see them!"

"Heh, Heh!" Chester chuckled then a "whoof!" as Joel, the six-year-old grandson by Jessie Mae and Carl barreled into him. "Where are you going in such a hurry?!" he asked, picking the boy up.

After dinner, in his den, Chester walked in and stopped. It was a photo above his desk that caught his eye.

Vietnam.

Chester remembered everything that happened. He was fine.

Some, like Harley Frakes, weren't.

Harley still woke up screaming about what happened. He'd gotten so addicted to heroin the dreams got worse, and finally ended it by waiting for a nice quiet evening to put a three fifty-seven magnum to his head and pulling the trigger.

Harley now lived in a home where he was spoon fed oatmeal three times a day, since nothing below his neck worked, and he couldn't taste anything anyway.

Then there was Richard Bates, one of the children whose parents killed themselves, but didn't take him with then. He already had a death wish. He got it granted in a swamp when a Vietcong AK-47 cut him in half. Chester got the gunner right when Richard died. There were more stories in his head, and he was glad he was writing them down.

Chester wouldn't let any of his friends who died be forgotten.

Damn the army and the government people who exploited their fears about discovery!

Now, none of it mattered.

All those years wasted.

Chester rethought that. No, they had been put to good use. They were that close to finding all of the answers, nearly done with mapping the complete human genome. They'd already had proven theoretical models for cloning.

All of that could benefit the world. All of it could go down in the dumper.

Chester looked to his left. The game table and its chairs sat in the corner with a Pente game on it. The game had been made in three dimensions, to give it more mental spice, as it were.

Going to the table, Chester had started a game, playing both sides. The outside world was red, the town blue. At its most basic, there were two ways to win. One, you put five of your color in a straight line, two, you captured five pair of your opponents color, a pair at a time.

The game was taking on a complex pattern of color, dating back to when the media first found out. It was interesting that both sides had two pair apiece. The lines were not complete, some of them having three, some two, none had enough to get five in a line.

He studied the table, then placed three pieces, two red, and one blue. "The next piece should be ours." He left, turning off the lights.

1968

Beale saw the young man who'd backed away in a hurry from him. Casually, he followed him. The young man was taking his time going wherever he was headed. Beale did everything he could to keep from being spotted. The one time he was spotted, he managed to make it look he wasn't doing what he was suspected of doing. He counted four, and then continued.

The young man finally went to a house in a, bless the luck! A secluded part of town. Beale crept quietly and undid the latch to the back yard, and entered. He swallowed, knowing just how wrong he was for being on the property uninvited. He barely choked down a gasp of amazement. The young man stood there shirtless and four armed. The double pupil eyes spotted Beale's reflection in the mirror. "DAMN YOU!" The youth shouted as Beale ducked down and broke away from the sight.

What he saw answered all questions.

By the time Dale Winters could get dressed, Beale was long gone. Dale knew it would take time for the stranger to get back to town on foot.

Beale made it back to their hotel room and roused Kiley. "We're getting out of here, now!"

"Yes . . . sir, but why?!" Kiley asked as he got his things and moved out with his commanding officer. Beale said nothing as they went to the front desk and paid their bill.

Beale glanced around and saw no unusual activity as they paid their bill. At their car, Beale said "get in, I'll drive." He pulled out the parking lot carefully, and then floored it. When they were a good twenty miles out of town, Beale finally explained what he saw.

"Sir," Kiley asked, "are you sure?"

"Son, we got out of there just ahead of the alarm." Beale said. "It only makes sense they would not want their men and boys going to war if it meant people finding out. I wonder how long they've been there."

"Well sir, it has to have been for a while. I wonder how many people like that are there." Kiley said.

"Good question." Beale said.

It took Beale and Kiley four months to convince their superiors they weren't crazy, another four to do a check on the place.

Ten months later, Beale and Kiley stood with others in a room in Atlanta facing a visibly furious Dale Winters. "Damn you. You just had to follow me, didn't you? Sneaking around my backyard," Dale sat shackled, after being lured to Atlanta by a letter from the army telling him he had to show up for the physical. He'd been double cuffed and dragged to an examining room, stripped and strapped to an examining table.

The next day, Dale found himself across a table in front of a single, bland looking man medium build, sandy hair and brown eyes. Nothing you'd remember.

"Good morning." Bland said as he'd sat down.

Dale merely stared, knowing someone was behind the one-way mirror behind bland.

"This can get easier if you cooperate." Bland said.

Dale snorted. "Yeah, right; all you guys are going to do is see that all of us are dead."

"Son," bland began.

"My father killed himself. You wanna join him?" said Dale.

"Why would your father kill himself?" Asked bland, taking the perceived opening.

"Look at what he got for a son. Thought God was punishing him."

Bland knew Dale was reluctantly telling what he knew, as did the others behind the one-way mirror. Bland would go slowly. "Is your mother still alive?"

"She's dead, too"

"Suicide..?"

"Yeah . . ."

"Do you know how this happened?"

"This what..?"

"Your four arms and double pupil eyes..?"

"Possible environmental pollution, most likely water borne . . ."

"How do you know this? I mean.... "

"I'm black? Or would you prefer colored? Nigger, perhaps...?" Dale arched an eyebrow.

Bland went red in the face. Dale liked that. "I meant no offense, but. . ."

"None taken; you're simply ignorant, so far."

Behind the one way, one of the brass said, "Got 'em big as church bells, don't he?"

A second replied, "You know what scares me? I don't think he's lying."

A third, "why do you say that?"

"He's not wavering, and he's damn sure it is the truth he's telling." The second said. "He may be right. We have to check out this town, what; Four Corners? See if what he says is true."

It didn't take the army long to confirm everything. Dale had apologized for what happened, and it took him a long time before he could look any one in the eye.

The army met with the town council in an open session. Everyone who could get in had at least one tape recorder going, and several secretaries had several steno pads at the ready. The army's representatives were amazed. There would be no misunderstandings about the price they would have to pay.

The deal was simple: one hundred and fifty young men would go to Vietnam. The town's knowledge of biology and chemicals would be available, and the government would keep their secret.

No one in town liked the deal, but no one could think of any other way out the situation.

NOW

Chester gazed at the photograph. Of the five men in it, two were dead, one lost his upper left arm, and he was the only one who walked away relatively unscathed. The cost of keeping the secret was too high, thought Chester. Not when it made the town resent the deal and lose some of its finest, most promising people.

Chester sighed, sat down and pulled one of his diaries from his desk. He turned it over, feeling the cracked and taped binding, running his fingers over its' worn page edges. Then he thought of Cody Macabee.

It was time to bring that one home.

The envelope originally created to keep the town from prying eyes was gone.

It was time to create a new envelope; one that would not break apart simply because of fear. No, this new one must stronger.

Chester put the diary away, then picked up a pen and paper and began to write.

15. INEVITIBLE FORCES

The next day at ten a.m., Mayor Mike Conners sat with Chester in his office. "I read over your ideas, Chester, but I have one problem. . ."

"What's that?" asked Chester, leaning forward.

"As you well know, requiring everyone to wear an unconcealed weapon might just be the trigger for some outsider idiot to really go off the handle. This we may not need to do."

"Maybe not, but after that jackass and his gang shot up the town, I say we should be ready for anything. It may be worse the next time, and we can't keep turning the other cheek. Pretty soon, all four will be bloody."

Connors rubbed his lips, a sure sign the mayor considered the idea seriously. "I don't like it. I keep hoping we'll come out of it okay, but we may not have a choice. I'll inform the rest of the council in, you present the idea."

"You could kill it by saying no right now, and I won't think the less of you for it. The alternative is to have the sheriff deputize more people." Chester told him. "Increase the patrols, just try and secure the town a little more."

Connors looked at him. "You try to keep them out, or us in?"

"Maybe a little of both," said Chester.

As this conversation was going on, the senior senator from Georgia, Sam Warner was holding a press conference. "I would like to thank all of you for coming on such short notice. As you all know, there is a town in my home state of Georgia called Four Corners. In it live people who have four arms and double pupil eyes. My problem is not with the people themselves, but why they would hide like this for so long. I am not calling for a full senate investigation of this place, just a full explanation of what happened so we can prevent it from happening again." He paused, looked up from his prepared notes. "Unlike some people who view them as freaks, I seem to understand their reluctance to say anything. I do not want their rights infringed upon, but I do believe we should find the underlying cause of this so we can all sleep. They have proven, in my mind, they are good citizens. We must respect that, and any wish they may have against exploitation of any kind, except that which they choose. It will take us all a while to get used to them. All I can say is, if Hollywood comes calling, get script approval." This brought laughter. "In all seriousness, we must ask the American people to remain calm, and do not make any unnecessary moves against them, and let us find out how this happened, and how it may be prevented in the future. I will now take questions."

"Will there be an attempt to sterilize them?"

"I don't think that will be an option, and the townspeople will have a great deal to say about it, most likely, no," was the reply.

"Will the government attempt to take over the town?"

"I don't believe that will be necessary."

"If there will be no controls on their breeding, what will stop them from trying to mate with normal people?"

The senator counted to three, and then said; "I don't believe they have any real interest in marrying outside of their town."

"If they change their minds..?"

"If the couple involve do mate by mutual consent, I don't think we have much to say about it. Besides, their silence for so long tells me they aren't interested in anyone from outside of town."

"Not interested, or haven't thought of it?"

"You must want to start a panic."

"Look, all I'm saying is what if they do want to marry normal people and have children?" The reporter stood his ground. "I think people have right to know if that can be prevented!"

"If you want to perform an act of genocide, you go right ahead. But I think the people of Four Corners will do everything in their power to stop you."

"Are you saying they should not any sort of supervision?" Another asked.

"I think they have supervised themselves quite nicely, without our help. What we need to remember is, we are the invaders there, and we should not overstep our bounds."

"Senator, is it true that the doctors and scientists examining Cody Macabee have stated they have found few variants from the norm?"

"Yes. They have found that whatever affected them rewrote the DNA patterns so that what was supposed to be twins, fused into a single being. They are still very much human." Sam Waters said. "These are good people who have served in the armed forces, who have made many successful efforts to care for our environment, and who are active in research in human DNA, starting with their own. They have made major discoveries that can benefit all of us. We should take advantage of it, and not, I repeat not make them objects of fear."

"Senator, like many other people, I realize they were afraid, they may still be afraid, but are you saying the government should do nothing at all?"

"I'm saying the government should not start putting anyone in a relocation camp when they've already done so for themselves. I think they kept their silence because they feared others' reactions."

"Do you believe there will be any restrictions on their movement?"

"Right now, no. But there will be a decision made on whether they can continue as they have. I think it isn't necessary."

"Many believe that their keep this secret is an act of deception. . ."

"Let me say this, it was a needed deception so they could move out in public. I believe there has been no harm done."

"Some people, including your fellow senators feel there harm has been done."

"To whom; I say they have been an asset, not a liability." Senator Warner said. "I will be going to Four Corners tomorrow to speak with the mayor. I hope we can find some peaceful resolution to this situation so no one's rights or their lives are unduly abridged. We cannot do this if we go off halfcocked." He gathered his papers and placed them in his pocket. "One of the cornerstones of this country is that all men are created equal, no matter what you look like. We aren't perfect at it by any means, but we can, at the very least, try not to 'punish' the people of Four Corners for what happened to them. Thank you for coming."

The gathered reporters watched as Sam Warner stepped away from the podium, their voices rising in a crescendo of questions, all of them knowing the senator just put his career on the line. They could see he was well aware of what he'd done.

In his car, Warner's assistant Mark Hamer stared at his boss. "You realize, sir, what you've just done?"

"Yeah," Warner said. "I've just taken up a possible unpopular cause."

"I just wanted to know if you realized that, Senator." Mark said quietly. "It's just that they scare me. . . ."

"You want to know a secret?" asked Warner.

"What?"

"My mom's from Four Corners. I was one of the few two armed babies born in the fifties. After that, my sister and my brother were born with four arms. They've spent their entire lives in Four Corners without incident until that asshole came in and shot up the town, and that moron televangelist came in trying to get people afraid of them."

"Maybe there's surgery, you know, to take off the extra two arms. . ." said Mark.

Warner smiled. "Do you know how much surgery would have to be done? You're talking about removing a major amount of skeleton and muscle, then replacing the bones. The body would never recover its ability to properly support itself. Besides, you want to ask them to remove something they now consider an asset? You might as well ask a sprinter to run on one leg."

Mark looked at his employer. "I didn't realize you knew so much about it."

"Biology was required in school. I also have a couple of degrees in environmental sciences and biology. You learn things because you need them. I love my siblings, Mark, and I will do what I can to protect them from exploitation. If that means taking on the scared and trying to teach them they're in no danger or knocking them back if they get stupid, then I will do it."

"You're in for a fight, sir," said his assistant.

"Tell me about it. We lose this; it just might be a bloodbath." Warner said.

Annamae and Luke Warner watched the press conference with pride. Their older brother had stood up for them. They and he knew the risks involved.

Annamae answered the knock at the door. Donnie Sanders, their neighbor came in at Annamae's bidding. "Y'all see Sam just now?"

"Yeah boy, I did!" Luke said. "I am proud of him. I just hope he can handle what's coming. They gonna try an' tear him apart."

Annamae beamed. "I taped it so we can play it back for him when he comes home in two days." She sat down; indicating Donnie should do the same. "I'm gonna use it in school tomorrow."

"Good idea." Luke said. "What do y'all think of Chester suggestin' everyone goin' around armed?"

"I don't know about that." Donnie said. "That just may be puttin' out a fire with gasoline. I think we should be ready, and maybe there should more people deputized, but I think we should hold the guns in check just a little while longer."

Luke responded; "my only problem with what you say is we should be ready for trouble. I think we should fight for our right to simply be alive. I won't lie to you, I'm scared."

"So is Chester," Annamae put in. "Personally, I think he's right. We need to be ready for anything."

Donnie nodded. "I just don't want us counter punching before a fist has been thrown, that's all. I don't want no escalation into a war."

Luke looked at his sister, then Donnie. "We may well be in one, and that rampage through town was only the first skirmish. It can get worse."

"I pray to God it don't." Donnie said sadly. "I saw enough death in Vietnam, thank you. I'll defend the town, that's sure. But I will not fire the first shot."

"Good enough." Luke said.

Joyce Madisen stood on the courthouse steps facing Phil and Jack.

"Ready?" asked Phil.

"To get it right; you better believe it." Joyce replied. "Let's do it."

"In at five-four-three-two. . ." Jack pointed at Joyce who began.

"I'm standing in front of the Four Corners courthouse here in Four Corners, Georgia. This town has been at the center of considerable controversy since the town has been revealed to the world." She walked to the bottom of the steps as she continued talking.

"The town has been an object of speculation and discussion ever since. Here are the facts: the local river water became polluted with a chemical soup that acted on the townspeople's DNA by forcing what should have been twins into four armed, double pupil people. These changes became dominant so that their children would have the same traits. We talked to Doctor Sam Murdock about it."

"I wasn't the one who really cracked it. It was a woman named Loraine Dozier, who found when she boiled water; there wasn't the usual residue in the boiler. It was a guess, really. When we analyzed the residue, then compared it with the chemical traces in the parent's and children's bodies, we found traces of the same chemicals."

"Don't you think it was strange that it was a lucky guess that put you on the right track?" asked Joyce.

"Not really. A lot of discoveries are made by accident, and I don't discount what Mama Dozier did just because she took a guess. It led us to our answers, and our new direction for the town."

"Doctor, do you think the government should do anything about the town now that you're known?"

"I think that people should realize there are no demons here, just a lot of good people who had something they didn't expect happen to them. It isn't the government's place to quarantine this town simply because these children turn out to be mutants. That is not a crime. I hope that there will be no more shoot ups of the town, but I doubt it will get better in the short run."

"Do you believe that a government takeover of the town is inevitable?" asked Joyce.

Sam Murdock took off his glasses, rubbed his eyes then put the glasses back on. "Yes. I have no doubt the government will try to order the sterilization of the townspeople. I would rather die than to let that happen." He took off his glasses and rubbed his eyes, then put them back on. "I have watched them grow up into good people. The argument that if they were good people, why would they hide is spurious. This town wanted to simply live its' life as best possible. I have spent thirty years seeing to that. I will not have it be for nothing."

"Does that mean you're willing to die for this town?"

"If it comes to that, yes," Sam said his voice firm. "I would die for this town."

The scene cut back to Joyce at the courthouse. "Sam Murdock has been the chief doctor in this town for some thirty years. His understanding of the mutations has made him a leading expert on DNA restructuring. His expertise will be called upon in an upcoming conference in Atlanta at the end of the month. He will also lecture at the University of Georgia later this month. Tomorrow, how they taught themselves to keep the secret."

"Great, Joyce." Jack said. "We'll do the intro to the next piece at the elementary school."

"Right," Joyce said her voice not quite sure. "I wonder if we're doing more harm than good."

"Trust me, we're doing some good," Phil said. "We got to remember we're the only ones right now who aren't just speculating. You may have missed out on the revelation of this town, but you're the only one who's getting to the bottom of everything."

"Phil's right. We may be the ones who favorably sway public opinion." Jack added. "I mean, the mutations may seem tragic, but you got to admit that they've done a damn good job of coping."

"Besides, you know how normal "normal" is. Why the hell should they be like us?" Phil said. He raised an eyebrow.

"Yeah; think about it. They're a lot stronger than we are. For them, it's personal, and they aren't gonna take any crap from us. That's why they're willing to die for each other." Jack said, helping Phil with his equipment to the van. "I think the only thing they really want us to do is tell the truth as we see it. Let's try and do that, okay?"

Joyce gave a nervous smile. "Okay. I just want this to go right. I want us to be right." She straightened her shoulders and managed to make her smile a little brighter. "Did we get permission to tape at the waste disposal unit?"

"Yeah, surprisingly," Jack said. "I didn't think they'd allow it, but we can go there tomorrow after we do the stand-up in front of the school."

"Okay. I guess the word is out we want to do a good job telling the story." Joyce said.

"Bet you get a Pulitzer." Phil said.

"It would be nice. . . ." Joyce sighed.

That evening, the network showed the report. The town was impressed. In Axle's bar, the patrons were talking.

"Whatcha think Axel?" Somebody asked.

"Not bad. I don't know if I like having the town exposed this way, but it beats having it shot up."

"Yeah," his waitress Mollie said. "My Joe still ain't recovered from that madness."

"How's he doing, Mollie?" asked Fred as he sipped from his beer.

"He's still having trouble sitting up, but the Doc says he'll be all right." She said.

"Who is treating him?" asked Farley.

"You know Larry Erhards' boy Vince?" Mollie said.

"Yeah, the one who broke my window with his baseball off the sand lot?" Farley asked. "Him..?"

"Yeah; he's good, you know. And he did pay for your window ten years ago. You ain't gonna let him forget it."

"I figure he at least owes me a checkup." said Farley as he took a drink from his beer, "Scared Mamie half to death."

"Mamie's always been scared half to death." Fred said quietly. "Hell, she gets scared when you break out the barbecue."

"Heh..! Y'all remember the time Jackie's boy Sam hit a homer that went into the upper bedroom and out the other window?"

Everybody laughed.

"Anyway, think these reports will do any good?" asked Fred. "I heard the mayor's cooperating with the reporter."

"Only 'cause she's the only one who hasn't made him sick to his stomach." Mollie said as she refilled a mug. "I understand Mike's taking her to the processing plant tomorrow to show her what we do there."

"What the hell for?!" asked Farley.

"I guess to show her what we do with the waste we take in. Didn't you hear Mollie?" spoke Fred. "I think it's a good idea. Might just calm more than a few folks down. Them that don't calm down can go to hell."

"I guess we can't stop it." Axel said as he took freshly cleaned mugs from the dishwasher. "Personally, I'm hoping that fool Devires get to go on trial unless someone kills him first."

"Oh, I'll be sad about that." said Farley. "I understand he's such a psychopath, his old man won't even help him."

"Devires, senior came to see his son, once. Left saying there was nothing he could say to him about what he did." Axel said as he finished putting the glasses away. An order came for a round of beer at a table. As he filled it, Axel said; "The judge set bail at one million dollars. Course, he caint make that kind of money come up, so he's still sitting there. Sheriff's put the word out no body touches him."

"Well, I understand how he feels. The last thing the town needs is a lynching. The safest place for him is in jail right now." Mollie said. "But I wouldn't mind taking a shot at him."

"You may be right, Mollie. About taking the shot, I mean." Fred drained his mug. "Well, I better get going. Wife will wonder where I am if I'm too late."

"Heh! Mamie wonders what's up if you're too early!" said Farley.

"Least mine worries." Fred returned as he left.

Farley stared at his mug. "I hope that reporter's stories help. . . "

Mollie wiped the place on the counter where Fred sat. "Truth usually does."

16. POSITIONING GAMES

It was hard enough that Peter Devires, Junior was going for his arraignment, but now he was being talked up as a hero by some of the more paranoid commentators.

Mac and Ronald Dennison sat in Kenny Cooney's house fuming at the television. "I cannot believe that bastard is a hero to some people." Cooney said through gritted teeth.

"I can." Ronald said. "I heard a song on the radio the other day about him. Jerk was a happy little pig cheering that maniac on. I'd like to show him what it's like to have your town shot up."

"Won't make no difference, Ronny." Cooney told him. "I was talking with the mayor. Says he's askin' the sheriff to see to it there's extra guards out in case someone decides to break him."

"Damn, Sam. We got to protect this trash so he can get to his trial…." Ronald said with disgust.

"Last thing we really need is for him to be a martyr." Mac said quietly. "I think we should go to the sheriff's station and register as deputies. Everybody's gonna be playing positioning games with this trail."

Peter Devires, Jr. was thrilled beyond words as he was led to the courthouse in a new, cheap suit. He watched as the crowds gathered around his car with the deputies and the heat and the signs and the chanting and the television cameras and the madness of spectacle. His palms were getting sweaty, and he wiped them on his pants. The three four armed men that guarded him and wore body armor kept neutral faces, but Devires knew they were raging inside. They spoke only if necessary, and they were doing their best to keep that to a minimum. The courthouse came up on their right and they turned into the parking garage behind it. There were more deputies brandishing riot guns and body armor with face masks. Those deputies had formed a line in front of the courthouse the length of the entire block it sat on.

"All of this for me?" Devires asked rhetorically.

The goad didn't work. They kept on until they got to the entrance they would use. At the entrance, there were more deputies along with a man in a suit. Devires got out and met him. "Peter Devires, Junior? I'm your court appointed lawyer, Max Schmelling. This will only be a hearing on the charges against you. They did read your Miranda rights to you?"

"Yeah, they did." Devires said. "Schmelling was the name of that boxer who lost to the nigger Louis?"

Schmelling stopped the procession dead. "Let's get something straight. I've got enough on you, including several outstanding warrants for various gun charges and assaults. The facts are these: even if you do walk on this, there are enough charges to put you in jail for a good long time. Don't antagonize your defender, okay?"

Devires gave him a mildly dirty look. "Yeah. . . ."

"By the way, smart mouth the judge, and everything goes. Got me?" Schmelling told him. "I just got your case. No matter what, I'm trying for an insanity plea to at least get you in a state mental hospital, but I doubt we'll get it."

The courtroom was packed and the murmur grew louder when the accused and his lawyer came in. The nondescript Schmelling sat down and pulled out his papers on Devires. "Is that all on me?" Devires asked, his eyes widening.

"Your old man must have pissed off somebody Chinese, 'cause you've had interesting times."

"All rise! The Honorable Judge William A. Stone presiding...."

Judge Stone was an imposing man, gray haired and distinguished; he had no nonsense demeanor and a steely eyed gaze that cut through anyone. "What do we have today, bailiff?"

"People versus Peter Devires, Junior, your honor."

Even Devires didn't like the look on the man's face.

"Is Peter Devires, Junior here?" Judge Stone asked sliding on a pair of glasses and looking over the papers the bailiff gave him.

"Yes he is, Your Honor." Schmelling said as he and Devires stood up. Devires rubbed his hands, glad to be rid of the restraints.

"The charges against you are: Murder, assault with intent to commit murder, reckless endangerment, and willful destruction of property. How do you plead?"

"Not guilty by reason of insanity, your Honor."

Stone took off his glasses. "You do realize how serious these charges are?"

"Yes we do, Your Honor." Schmelling said. "I believe I can prove my client was not in his right mind at the time."

Stone wore a sour look. It was gonna be one of those cases. "I see. Very well, then, this case begins in three weeks with jury selection. I will let you know in advance there will be no switching of venues, period. Is that understood?"

To his credit, Schmelling didn't let his disappointment show. "We understand, your Honor. Three weeks."

The town was on tether hooks, with many visibly armed with guns on their hips. Children were picked up by their parents from school and the playgrounds were empty.

"The silence is palatable here in Four Corners." Joyce Madisen said as the camera panned past empty schoolyards. "Ten inch thick shutters cover the windows of this school house and the insides are lined with sheet steel now. The children understand, and the greatest tragedy is that their childhoods are being stolen. The runs to the waste processing plant have four guards now. The entire way of life here is severely affected by this trial. They won't say it on camera, but they know if Peter Devires Junior walks, he won't have time to gloat. According to one townsman who spoke off the record, Devires is dead either way." The camera was now on Joyce.

"The facts are simple; this case represents their very worst fears come true." She said. "Four Corners is expecting something to happen, and soon."

Tourists still came, as if wanting to be in the epicenter of the explosion. They still gawked and pointed, ate at the diner, drove to the processing plant just to stare at it from outside of the gates. The research lab was a stop of course, and they came in droves, some taking pictures, happiest when they got a shot of a guard in full body armor.

The government came by, finally admitting they knew about the town and denying they were the cause of the mutations. The government even awarded a contract for research jobs from top secret to the mundane. They also got their own scientists into the laboratories since the town felt this was the first step to a possible takeover, and they subscribed to the notion you hold your enemies closer. Some were grateful the suspicion was mutual, even if it made the workplace tense.

The government scientists were surprised at the amount of security, even if they should have expected it. Before they came in, complete background checks were made, back several generations, DNA samples were taken, along with retina scans and fingerprints. The scientists found the Four Corner scientists knew more about them than their nominal employers.

The government wanted to post National Guardsmen in the town, but the answer was no. "We protect our own," said the mayor.

It happened two days before the trail was to start.

It was the few who'd escaped from the first rampage.

They found the money somehow to get re-equipped and more vehicles.

Four of them went on a rendezvous with the car taking Devires to the courthouse.

They lay in wait, at least three blocks from the courthouse.

The car made its' way from the jail, with its' armed escort. Number one was at the first corner the car had to turn and fired at the tires, hitting the left rear as planned. The driver managed to control the skid and brought the car to a halt. The other three sprinted to the stopped vehicle and pointed wicked looking weapons at the occupants, ordering them out. The four four-armed men got out, hands rose. They were ordered to their knees and to take off their headgear. One of them got the keys and undid the cuffs. Devires looked at his former captors with the deepest contempt, pulled of the of the guard's shotgun and placed it against the guard's head and pulled the trigger. Soon, all four guards were dead, their brains and blood splattered on the ground and their blood mingling in a red pool on the road.

That evening, the news screamed its headline story of the dead guards and showed the agony of the town.

The nation knew those men were dead if the townspeople caught them.

Peter Devires, Junior fled to the west.

The manhunt was on.

"All right, let's get this meeting together!" Mayor Connors said, banging his gavel on the table. "We all know what happened with that bastard Devires getting away from his escort and his well-deserved trial. I have no doubt that he will try something when the heat dies down. I also have no doubt that we now have to make some changes to how we do things around here. We no longer have the luxury of secrets, and we cannot go back to the way we were any more than our parents could."

"Everything changes, Mayor." Mama Dozier said calmly from her wheelchair. "That does not mean we have to live in fear. If he shows up again, we will take care of him. But we have to be sure of ourselves before we allow panic and paranoia set in. Y'all are known, now, and you have to deal with that. You dealt with what you are, you're now gonna have to deal with these changes. That's the only constant, change."

The filled room's eyes were on the highly respected woman in the wheelchair. Randall Pearson stood up. "I agree with Mama and the Mayor. I say we rebuild our home. I say we don't let that bastard win, not like this. I'm not lying down to die for the bigots in this world. We were here a long time, and I say that if we weren't supposed to exist, the first of us would have died when they were born."

This was met with cheers and shouts of "AMEN!" "DAMN STRAIGHT!" "WE REBUILD!" "THIS IS OUR HOME! NOBODY"S GONNA CHASIN' US FROM HERE!"

The Mayor nodded his head in approval. He smiled at Mama Dozier. "I guess we'll rebuild. All right, let's see what we have in the way of supplies. . . ."

Kenny Winston stood up. "As you know, my lumber yard will supply whatever y'all need. We'll arrange payment later. I'm glad we're fightin' for ourselves."

The crowd gave its agreement, and plans were made to improve and beef up the town's security. The omnipresent television camera sent the meeting out.

In Washington, the president made low interest loans available. To most everyone's surprise, the loans were barely touched.

"We're grateful the president saw fit to offer the loans," Conners said warmly, "but we feel it's best to do as much as we possibly can to fix the mess ourselves. As long as they're available, fine. But we would like to see what we can do first."

The town went back to repairing itself, and Joyce Madison's reports continued.

But unease was building. People could feel it, but they just couldn't name it.

One home had been torched while the owners were away.

Another had been torched, but the owners weren't so lucky, being overcome by the smoke and dying by immolation.

Rennette Murphy and her husband Mason were coming home from a movie when they saw a van firing something at their two-story house. The couple could do nothing but watch the house go up in flames almost instantly. To their horror, the van's occupants spotted them, the back door opened and a nozzle or a muzzle pointed at then. The couple's wits returned quickly once they realized what was going on, and they started to run. The van accelerated toward them firing.

"Split up!" Mason yelled, his wife running to the left, he to the right. Rennette made it to an alley that had trashcans and cars in it. She dove under one and prayed. The van flew by her. She counted ten, making sure she no one coming and ran in the same direction, praying the occupants of the van didn't stop at the other end.

Luck was with her and she ran down the street to a neighbor's house. Banging on the door, she screamed; "HELP ME! PLEASE, HELP ME!"

The door flew open and the man who answered asked her; "WHAT"S GOING ON HERE?!"

"I saw who been torchin' the houses!" Rennette said. "They came after us, and me and Mason split to keep them from gettin' us both! I saw 'em! I know I did!"

The man pulled her inside as she spoke, and turned off the lights. "You saw 'em?"

"Yeah," Rennette said, trembling like a leaf in a hurricane.

Her rescuer dialed the sheriff. "We got a witness to the torch. They may still be in town. Get the helicopters up. We may be able to spot them from the air." He hung up the phone.   "Mazie, get our witness her to the sheriff's station. I'm going to get the rest of the boys on our block team, and start lookin' for that van."

"You know it was a van?" asked Rennette.

"Yeah, we do. We just didn't have a live witness until you came here. The man who died in the second fire told us before he died he'd seen a van and a face before they shot his window with whatever they used to start the fire. He fought his way out of the coma to tell us, and then gave up after he said what he'd seen. I want these bastards." He kissed Rennette's brown forehead. "We gonna get 'em."

It took less than two minutes for the four helicopters to get in the air. Splitting to the four winds, the one going to the east spotted the van and alerted the deputies. "They do not get away, you hear me?!" Jim Mosley growled into the mike. "I want them caught; if they get killed, too bad. I'm tired of every wacko using us as a scapegoat for what makes 'em shit in their pants."

"We've spotted 'em, sheriff! They headin' toward the 5-7! I repeat the 5-7! We don't catch 'em. . . "

"We hear you! We're on our way!" Mosley said. "Set up the road block before they get to Irwinton! I don't want them gettin' away!"

Satch Maybert spotted them in his car and gave pursuit. He was joined by three other cars, all of them running flat out. The van was doing its' best to outrun the relatively sleeker cars, but it was a losing battle. The rear of the van opened up, pointing the nozzle of it's' weapon at it's' pursuers. "Watch it, boys, that's the thing that torched the houses!"

"They can't do it from the side and rear car they?" asked Frank Taylor in his Camaro.

Satch pointed powerful quartz light at the van. "It's on a pivot!"

"Good! They may have a radio scanner. I think we all know what we got to do…." Frank said.

"If they roll and tumble, tough!" Satch said. "But be careful, that stuff they're using may be strong enough to burn your car!"

Just then, the helicopter dropped to the road in front of the fleeing van; the driver swerved, running off the road and tumbling into a ditch, landing in its' roof. The pursuing cars came to screeching halts next to the stopped vehicle.

"Are those sons of bitches alive?!" Somebody asked.

"I hope so. I'd love to kick their ass…." another said.

Mosley drove up, along with a camera crew. "Sorry about the press boys, but you know they were following me."

"We ain't blaming you…." Satch said, pointing. "They're down there; by the book?"

Mosley nodded. "This is Sheriff Jim Mosley. We have you surrounded. Come out with your hands up." No answer. Mosley glanced at his assembled deputies. "Approach with caution; I want no loss of life on our side."

The deputies slowly approached the disabled van, fanning out in a circular pattern. Their weapons drawn, led by Satch who went to the rear doors of the van and opened one and looked in. The news crew could see him shake his head slowly. "Forget it, sheriff. Ain't no need for a rush."

Mosley joined him, the reporter right behind him. Mosley looked in, shook his head, saying, "Just call the coroner to come pick up the bodies. They won't be torching anyone else's home again."

"Sheriff, do you think they're part of a group out to eradicate your people?" The reporter asked as they made their way back to the road.

"They ain't anymore," was all Mosley would say.

"Do you believe this will bring an end to the attacks on the town?"

"No I don't. People are scared of us, even if we haven't done anything to warrant it."

"There is talk the federal government might impose a quarantine on the town."

"Real bright idea, ain't it?" Mosley said with disgust. "We've already quarantined ourselves. I could quite happily go back to that."

"Do you believe the rest of the country should relax, you're not coming for their children?"

Mosley had enough, but he figured to give her a solid sound bite. "Look, as far as I'm concerned, if the rest of the country is that scared of us, they can go to hell. Since they're so afraid of us, I'd say they're already there." He got into his car and drove away, allowing Satch to take over.

17. ROLL OF THE DICE

Rennette Murphy looked at the broken van on the trailer after it had been brought from the crash site. "That's it."

"You sure?" asked Jim Mosley as they watched the investigation team go over it for fingerprints.

"I'm very sure that's the van. I'll never forget it chasing me like it did. I'm glad Mason got away, too. I don't know what I'd do without him. . ."

"I know how you feel." Mosley said. "The four punks in the van didn't have any identification on them. Heh, wonder why?"

"Oh, sure, you wonder," said Rennette. "You gonna call me later about this, right?"

"If we need you," Mosley put his upper right arm on her shoulder and squeezed. "If there's anyone else stupid enough to pull this kind of stunt, they will find us ready for them."

"I don't like living like this." Rennette said, fury edging her voice. "What we really need to do is nail one of the trash doing this in front of the cameras instead of them coming after it's all over."

"Honey, that's the way it normally happens." Mosley told her. "Cain't be helped."

"That's cold comfort," said Rennette sadly. "I'm going to the shooting range with Mason today. I finally agreed to do it, even if I don't like guns. I don't know if I'll feel any safer, but I'll least know how to handle one."

"I understand, believe me." They walked to the station house, with Mosley feeling her lower left hand in his lower right. "You gonna be all right?"

"No. I ain't gonna be all right ever again. The rest of the world knows we're here, and we cain't go back to the way we were. I don't like it, and there's nothing any of us can do about it." Tears welled up in her eyes and she buried her head on his shoulder. Behind his mirrored glasses, Jim Mosley felt his own tears break through and they flowed with hers. He quickly used his upper hands to wipe his eyes. It wasn't that he was ashamed to cry, he rather do it in private.

The wind was starting to gust, and the rain began to fall. Mike Conners, the mayor of Four Corners sat in his office looking out his window, trying to make any kind of sense of it all. They'd kept their secret for so long, and he'd liked it that way. There were no troubles from outsiders, and now all of this . . . this . . . mess.

Callie's fried chicken sat on his desk, still warm from the quick zap he gave it in the office's microwave, along with fresh mashed potatoes and cooked in the microwave vegetables. A slice of her peach pie and fresh biscuits and coffee rounded out the meal.

He dug in and thought about what had to be done to keep the town safe.

It was impossible now that they were known. No matter how much they wished it different, they couldn't go back to the relative peace and quiet of the good old days.

The government was in town for good, no doubt about it, and no arguments. The town council had long since begun a search downriver to see if there were others who were affected by the chemicals as was Four Corners. They had turned up at least a dozen corpses, and many more people who'd been told they'd been punished by God for some unknown sin. Many of those people moved to Four Corners, happily leaving their old pain behind and allowing those who knew them where they went. If not forget them, at least they would not be able to shun them.

Conners followed a bite of vegetables and potatoes with a drink from the coffee. Too much was at stake, most of all their freedom. The town would not give up without a fight that much was sure. Conners smiled at that thought.

The senior senator from Georgia watched the screen as the images from Four Corners came across the screen as the junior senator sat next to him. The two men could see the possibilities of this town and its' people, they could also see the possible backlash.

"I want to know something." The senior senator said.

"What is it?" asked the junior senator, shifting in his seat.

The senior senator faced him. "How did you feel when you found out about your brother and the others?"

The junior senator had expected this. "I was a little scared at first, and then I realized he wasn't a threat to me if I wasn't a threat to him. I was right. We're very close." He took a drink from his glass. "Look, he was my older brother. He was a lot of fun, and he never made me feel bad because I didn't have four arms, like him."

The senior senator's eyes left the screen and looked at his junior, hard. "Let me make this very clear. We have been asleep on this because one hand didn't know what the other was doing. You've stepped into the hell pit of public opinion over this, and there are a lot of people who'd feel better if you denied all of this. I don't know if I can back you up on this."

"Look, I knew what I was doing when I admitted my ties to my hometown. I will not deny any of that, just to make some people happy." The junior senator said. "I will admit we kept it secret just because of this sort of uproar. The town will not go back into its' shell, senator, and I will not see it forced back into it." He paused. "Look, I am fighting for my hometown, surely you can see that?"

"I see it, son. But do you see what it can cost you?" The senior senator said. "What about your career in congress?"

"Do that at the expense of my family and friends? Congress can go to hell." The junior senator said. "I don't give a damn about congress if it costs me my family and friends. I've known them far longer than I've known you. If you think I'm going to let you or anybody else makes them eat shit and howl at the moon without a fight, you're crazy."

The senior senator gave a slow smile. He'd liked this younger man, and now he knew why. "I'll back you as far as I can, but you will be going down in the mud for this one."

"Hey, let's get dirty." The junior senator said. "I'm ready as I'll ever be."

A bomb blew up a bar and the bomber was trying to get away in his car. Someone gave chase and rammed his car into the bomber's car. The crowd that gathered dragged him out of the car, and the news cameras caught a vicious beating in time for the evening news. The sheriff's deputies stepped in and got him to a local hospital.

They kept him alive with great reluctance.

The next day, protesters marched on the town demanding the assailants be brought to justice. The town shouted back, wanting to know why these outsiders thought they hadn't done anything wrong, and what was wrong with defending your town anyway?

The mayor said that everything was being done to find them, but there weren't enough deputies on the force to go searching for the assailants. "We will look at the video tape, but I doubt if we can make it stick one any one person."

The question of whether the town was all that interested in finding the attackers was offered.

The reply was why that fool had to come to their town anyway.

The war of words escalated as the town made a show of being armed.

It would get worse.

A deputy was attacked.

A tourist was laid prone on the ground after being found with a gun.

The elementary school was pelted with rocks from a moving car.

Someone snuck into the rear of the diner while the evening crew was busy with the evening rush and stole food from the refrigerator.

Two teenagers were caught breaking into a house and were wounded by the occupants in the legs with bullet wounds.

Mike Conners called a press conference and read a statement. "All trespassers will be shot on sight if they are caught, and legal council will be provided for those doing the shooting free of charge, the plea being self-defense. If the attacks on this town do not stop, we will not be responsible for our actions in our own defense. Enough is enough. We will no longer tolerate this madness brought down on us simply because of what we are. All actions in our defense are now justified because these individuals or groups have decided no one will care about us. This is patently false. We care about ourselves, and the kid gloves come off, now. This is your last warning. Your asses are grass, and we have the lawnmowers, and the weed whackers are set on high. You take your lives in your own hands when you attack us, and you have no excuse for your actions. That ends the statement. That is it."

"The Mayor of Four Corners has tossed down the gauntlet to any outsiders willing to cause trouble here." Joyce Madisen said afterwards. "The tension has become unbearable for a formerly peaceful town. Patrols have been stepped up; the citizenry has been authorized to use deadly force if necessary. We will see if the bomber was the only time that will happen, or will it lead to brutal deaths in a formerly quiet town; This Joyce Madisen, Four Corners, Georgia."

It soon came to a head. Four men in another van were flying through the town center firing machine guns. Toddy Hampton gave chase along with five others in their car. Toddy braved the gunfire and rammed the van sending it into a pole. The pursuers caught up with them. The four refused to give up and were riddled with bullets. The bodies were displayed in a glass booth in city hall.

The relatives protested as they were refused permission to take possession of the bodies amid taunts from the townspeople.

The town was giving as good as they got, and no one outside of it liked it. The freaks weren't gonna take it, period.

The president sat at the conference table surrounded by advisers.

"Let me tell you that this situation in Four Corners is getting way out of hand. No matter what happens, we'll get the blame for letting this go on too long. I need suggestions." The president said, visibly agitated.

"Mr. President, I can think that the temporary solution is to put the National Guard there, until the situation calms down." One man said. "Let me be honest, sir. I find them . . . unnerving sir."

"You think I don't?" The president replied. "I'll be honest. They scare me, too. But no matter what we personally think, and no matter whether or not some would approve if we let them go down in flames, none of us are gonna let that happen, and the last thing any of us want to see is that town a smoking ash heap on our watch. We don't want to give our enemies comfort by letting this go on. Now the governor and I have had a long talk, and he's willing to put the guard in, but he wants to know if he has back up. I've assured him he does."

"What if the townspeople don't trust us, sir?" The same man said. "We could lose a lot on this."

"We can lose a lot more than just face. The facts are simple. One: the people of Four Corners simply want to be left alone. Two: If we don't help them out, can you imagining the worldwide repercussions over this? I can just hear the preaching about how we don't have our own house in order over human rights. I don't need that, period. Three: do you really want to see that town sitting at its' borders waiting for the first stranger to come in so they can pick them off? I don't think so." The president's people glanced at each other. One by one, they nodded their heads in agreement.

"Fine," the president said, "Let's get to work."

18. DANCE OF THE MUTANTS

The National Guards were in town, now.

The violence, for the most part, stopped.

This meant almost nothing to the townspeople. The general feeling was they still had to protect themselves.

Try as they might, the town would not relax.

That Sunday, the Reverend Jacob McCandless stood at the pulpit's microphone. His voice was full of righteous indignation as he spoke. "You know, brothers and sisters, ever since we were discovered, other people have been debating our fate." He laughed, shaking his head. "Outsiders who rush to judgment of people who were right to be wary of them, people who were right to hide what made them different from the rest of the world. It seems to me, 'Judge not, lest ye be judged" is a perfect topic this morning. I have been wondering, how to approach the subject. I've been wondering, how to say what was on my mind."

"Amen's," came from the congregation, which included the media, as usual these days.

"It is hard, for people without our features to understand why we said nothing to the outside world. I need only to point out to you the sterilization of the mentally challenged; I think that is the correct phrase these days, to you."

Again, there was a chorus of "amen" from the congregation.

"I need only point out the sexually transmitted disease experiments that were done on black men at Tuskegee."

The shouted amen came louder and horde this time.

"I need only point out to you the atrocities done, in the name of science to the Jews in the concentration camps in World War Two!"

There were loud, raucous "Amens" this time as several members stood to their feet and shook their fists in the air.

"I want to ask you, brothers and sisters, what would they have done to us in the late nineteen forties and early fifties?" McCandless looked his congregation in its' collected eye. "At a time when blacks in the south had to march just so they could ride the bus like human beings, when the communist scare was at its' greatest height, these people outside of our little town want to know why we didn't tell 'em!?" He reached in his pocket, pulled out a dollar and said: "Here's a dollar, buy the clue!" This brought a round of applause and laughter. "At a time like that, when don't know what's going on, but you can't bring yourself to trust anyone outside of those that know, it is important that you steel yourself to find out for yourself. This town took it upon itself to learn about the changes wrought in our bodies." He held up his four hands, the congregation stood and did the same. "For those of you who are two armed, and that's most of you, this is a frightening sight. But what we are, mothers and fathers, sons and daughters, sisters and brothers uncles and aunts, grand mothers and fathers. We are doctors and lawyers, teachers and students, poets and painters, preachers and planters. In short, we are everything you are." McCandless stared right at the cameras, as if he was fixing the world with his gaze. "All we are trying to do is live our lives the best way we know how. If we are here, it is because we are meant to be here, and nothing you can do, including our deaths will change that. We will fight you with everything we have. Or you can choose to deal with us peaceably. We will not throw the first blow, but we will throw the last." He smiled. "The Lord, you see, is my shepherd, too." McCandless placed his hand on the huge bible on the podium. "To my brothers and sisters, I say this: the Lord puts no more on us than we can carry, even in this world. Today is communion Sunday, and I want you to all think about this: if we were not meant to be here, we would have died in childbirth. I want you to think about that. I would like the choir to sing for me, 'The old Rugged Cross' as the Communion is prepared. Seems to be appropriate right now," The broken crackers and sweet wine were passed through the congregation as everyone too theirs and passed the rest on. When all had received their portion and the small plastic cup of wine, barely bigger than a half shot glass, the Reverend Jacob McCandless lifted the cracker up, saying: "this the body of Christ," he placed it in his mouth, the congregation doing the same. Then he lifted the cup of wine saying, "This, the blood of Christ," then drank. "Let no man take falsely of the body and blood of the Lord." He gave the cup to a waiting deacon. "As we leave the sanctuary, remember, if we walk with God we need fear no man. If we have faith, we need not fear the world, for what harm can it do us?" McCandless raised his hands. "May you walk with Jesus all the days of your life, May he keep and protect you, even unto your darkest hour, and at the time of your passing, may he receive you in his bosom. May all the blessing of God be with you all the days of your life…"

He stepped from the pulpit and walked to the front of the church, shaking hands.

The churches of Four Corners were letting out and the worshipers milled around allowing the sun to warm them. The comment weren't on the sermons they'd heard as National Guard trucks rumbled through the town.

Children watched as the Guardsmen tried not to stare at them and failed. One boy, Carlton Morrow walked up to a Guardsman and looked up. To the six year old, the man was huge, as he was decked out in full riot gear. The boy walked around him, sizing him up. The face of the Guardsman was watching the boy as he looked over his companion. The boy's father watched out of the corner of his eye.

"Are you hot in that?" asked Carlton as he looked up at the guard.

"Yeah, I am," said the guard. "Aren't you supposed to be with your parents?" He added nervously.

"They're over there," Carlton said, pointing at his parents. "As long as they can see me, it's okay."

"I don't know if it would really be okay. You're not supposed to talk to strangers, are you?"

"No, but you're here to protect the town, right?" asked the boy.

The guardsman was taken aback. "Well, yeah. . . ."

"Then you're not that strange." said Carlton. "My name's Carlton. What's yours?"

The guardsman glanced over at his counterpart, who smirked a little at his companion's predicament. "Corporal Mac Davison, son...."

Carlton gave him a salute. "It's nice to meet you, Corporal."

"Carlton, get over here and stop bothering that man!" His father said as he came over to get the boy. "I'm sorry...." He looked at the insignia, "Corporal, but he's been excited ever since you came into town. I don't know why." He smiled, and then held out his hand. "I'm Jack Morrow. This is Carlton. I'm sorry if he bothered you."

"Corporal Mac Davison. It's no bother, but something happens, and the boy could get hurt."

"Believe me, I understand. I hope you understand how nervous we are. There aren't too many of who are happy you have to be here." Jack told him.

"I can tell you I'm not too happy myself." Davison said. "Let's face it, I mean you guys do look pretty weird to a lot of people, me included."

Jack smiled. "I got news for you. Most of us don't have any interest in taking over the place. I've got a family to raise...."

The guardsman laughed. "Me, too," He sobered up. "Look, I still don't know what to think of you people...."

"Fine by me as long as you think for yourself," interjected Jack.

"I guess I'm just... I don't know....Oh hell, I don't know! I mean, suddenly, here we are living a science fiction movie, and nobody knows what the hell to do about it!" Davison said.

Jack Morrow could see the frustration was eating at the Guardsman. He felt sorry for him, and his fellows. All this was confusing, and the leaders of the country weren't helping. "Look, I don't know what to say to you. We've lived here all our lives in peace. It's you that are the intruders, not us. If there's any trouble, it will be from outside of the town. I think you should know that. We're good people. Remember that." He took Carlton's hand. "Years ago, my Daddy told me there would be Hell to pay once the outside world found out about us. He was right. Only, it ain't happened yet." He started for his wife standing near the church.

"When do you think Hell starts around here?" Davison asked.

Jack Morrow looked around at his friends and the guardsmen. "Soon enough," He went to his wife with his son, took her hand, squeezed it, and then walked home.

The motorcade drove the main drag, the occupants of the car taking in as much of the town as they could. President James Dalton and his wife, Terry Morton Dalton, sat in the awe of how much the town kept its' small town feel, despite having one of the most advanced chemical industries in the country. It was all part of the art of concealment the town had mastered. The junior senator from Georgia, Sam Warner, rode with them.

The president looked at the crowds watched his motorcade go by. "You know Sam; I look at these people, and find it hard to believe you come from here."

"Well, I do come from here Mr. President, and I'm proud of it." Warner told him.

"I didn't mean anything by it. I just mean, why you don't have four arms?" said the president.

"I guess it skipped me and did my brother instead." Warner replied. "I never had a problem with it, since we knew others it happened to. It's a mutation, not a disease. If you're uncomfortable, we can always go back. After all, they will see you're nervous."

"Son, anybody would be nervous." President Dalton said. "That is normal. What I'd like to do is assure the town this president will not be putting anyone one in a concentration camp."

"All I know, sir, is that we place ourselves in isolation for our own protection. I think we made the wisest choice. But that's over now, and the job is to make sure that life can go on here. I grateful you could do this."

"I won't lie to you Sam. I was advised not to do this." President Dalton said. "You don't know how close I came to staying put."

"I realize that sir. I was advised it was a bad idea to ask you." Warner returned. "But I had to try."

"I know, Sam. So did I," Dalton said, glancing at his wife. "As a matter of fact, Terry pointed out; it would make me look cowardly if I didn't do it. I agreed."

"Thank you ma'am," Warner said.

"Not a problem. I thought it was all getting out of hand, anyway. What better way to promote a little calm than by going to the town?" Terry Morton Dalton was a handsome woman, all strong features with deep, intelligent eyes. "I felt even if the townspeople kept their secret, it wasn't ours to second guess them."

"Thank you again." Warner saw they were coming to city hall. He could see Mayor Conners along with the town council standing on the front steps. A red carpet was laid out, and the path cordoned off. There was a police line with deputies spaced about every ten feet or so, forming a protective shield.

The presidential limo stopped in front of the steps, and a cheer rose from the crowd as the president and first lady got out, followed by Warner. The trio walked up the steps and the Mayor extended his hand to the President then the First Lady.

"Welcome to Four Corners, Mr. President." Conners said.

"It's good to be here." Dalton said as he waved to the crowd. "I've wanted to do this. You've managed to keep the town feeling like a small town."

"We pride ourselves on that, Mr. President, First Lady." Conners said. "If you'll come this way....?"

Suddenly, Conners heard the shot and stood in front of the first couple. The slugs hit him square in the chest and he went down in a heap. The deputies pulled the president and first lady into the building quickly, while the crowd scattered and the deputies ran in the direction of the shots.

"There's the bastard!" an excited shout came as a figure was spotted running toward a waiting car. Another car turned on the street. The driver saw what was going on and floored the accelerator and rammed the car. The driver of the rammed car slammed his head against the steering wheel and slumped in the seat. The driver of the car that rammed him pointed a forty five out of his shattered window, and fired.

The gunman, hit in the leg, wisely surrendered as the furious deputies pointed everything they had at him, praying they would have an excuse to kill him outright.

Conners was rushed to the hospital, barely alive. The doctor fought to keep one of their own alive, even as the President and First Lady were rushed back to Washington.

The next morning, Doctor Martin Feldon broke down as he told the waiting reporters that Mike Conners, the Mayor of Four Corners, died from his wounds.

The town mourned of course, and its anger grew at the outsider who did this. Their pain was such that the town was, for all intents and purposes, closed off. If it had been hard to talk to the town's people before, now it was near impossible. Any two armed person was seen with the utmost suspicion, and at the local clubs, if they were let in, they needed three pieces of identification, and some who knew them to vouch for them and take responsibility. Needless to say, no one from outside got in.

Even the diner, which offered the warmest welcome, iced up. The waitress took to wearing a gun on her hip; with a shoot first, ask questions later policy firmly in place.

Even the school children froze up. Unless they knew the two armed children, those children weren't welcome.

The president of the town council, Brett Masterson, told the world they were no longer welcome in Four Corners. This brought a swift response from both media and government.

"This tragedy should not cause the people of Four Corners to isolate themselves in their pain. I share with them the loss since their courageous mayor Conners gave his life to protect mine and the first lady's lives. They should not turn away in fear and anger from the rest of the world in their suffering. They should, if they can, find the strength to forgive the assailant, and not use this as an excuse to shut out their fellows." President Dalton was still visibly shaken from the attack, and did his best to make it clear that he was on their side. "I will make another trip to Four Corners. I would like you all to remember that not everyone is against you, and that many people admire you for your courage, your strength, and your willingness to grow despite everything that has happened to you. You demonstrate what this country is all about in the first place. Terry and I will be there for the funeral. After such a sacrifice, it's the least we can do to show our respects."

Some said it was appropriate the day of Mike Conners funeral dawned grey and overcast.

Conners had overseen some the most intense development of the town, including the waste processing plant that rendered a great deal of toxic chemicals inert. He saw to their schools stayed among the best in the world. Despite his easy going manner, his was one of the keenest minds in a town that prided itself on its' scholastic achievements. He even held several patents in chemistry, and spent much of his free time teaching.

At the funeral, these memories and more were brought out, and through the tears, the laughter rang out. They showed the video of him cutting the ribbon to the first phase of the waste treatment plant, with his children, and giving a speech;

"It is my hope, that one day we can take our place in the larger community of this state, the nation and the world. I must remind you of how far we've come, and how far we have to go. I have no doubt that when we are found out by the public at large, we will face trouble, and we will face difficult times. I have no doubt we will meet the challenges with all the dignity and courage we have. Our strengths are many, and I think we all know where we have to improve. I believe we will meet and beat the challenge. Even if I don't get to go with you into whatever future awaits. My love and respect goes with you. I love you all, you are my family, and nothing will even change that, not even my death."

Thomas Conners, the eldest son stood up with his three siblings, Calli, Jake and Markham. Thomas began singing his father's favorite hymn, his siblings adding their voices to his.

Conners had been mayor twice, and was a sure bet for re-election. Many felt a hole had been punched into the life of the town. There were many two armed people in the church, and they were to the townspeople's' eyes, were just as shocked as they were, and their sympathy seemed genuine. They filed past the casket, looking down onto the face of a man who showed the kind of courage they wished they could show. Some broke, realizing exactly what was going on here. This town was fighting for its' life, and now one of it's' warriors was gone. Even the media was far more subdued than anyone had a right to expect, trying to keep their commentary dignified, and their voices low. Some of them had interviewed Conners before his death, and many of them liked him. They did what they could to provide background on a man that none of them really knew.

Joyce Madison came through again. "Michael Henry Conners was one of the original four armed children, born in nineteen forty-eight. He was raised by 'Mama" Irene Dozier, the woman who found the cause of the children's' mutation. He went on to college and several degrees, among them chemistry, and government. He oversaw the most extensive development of the town and its' resources. A teacher as well as an inventor who held several patents in multiple disciplines he was a quiet spoken man with a keen mind and sharp wit. I had the pleasure of interviewing him for some of my first reports from Four Corners. I had a feeling he was the man to really lead the town fully out in the open. That will still happen, but how is the question. As for me, I always thought, in the short time we talked, he was looking farther ahead than anyone. He could see something I couldn't, that most of us would miss. I think that he must have seen just how good it could be. But now, he'll never know. This is Joyce Madisen from Four Corners."

19. MAYBE IT'S JUST ME

It was two days after Mike Conners' funeral. The town for once was quiet, almost somber. There seemed to be no lifting the emotional haze that had settled and everyone agreed something had to be done, some forward motion achieved. There seemed that everything they'd worked for had turned to dust, blown away by a hurricane of hate and fear.

Even the diner wasn't immune. What had been a friendly, warm place had fallen into to sullen silence, almost unbreakable.

Jimmy Robertson was not a little happy about this. On his show, the Spirit Club, he gleefully pointed out how the town had brought it on themselves, and that there was no excuse any more, that no defense could be made for the inhabitants of Four Corners. "Oh yes!" He shouted with glee, "they could pelt me with all the manure they want to, but God will not be mocked! Their downfall was inevitable! This was meant to be, period!" His audience applauded and cheered, and he was safe there. It still stung that he'd been bombarded by feces and urine, the shit literally hitting his fan. But the death of the mayor that challenged him, that had to be a sign. It had to be. "The Godly shape of man will reign again; the hero who shot that freak of obscene, perverted nature will be freed from an unjust prison. We are raising funds for his defense. Should the jury, somehow be conned or cowed into convicting him, we shall do our best to get his release from prison."

Marcy watched as her VCR recorded the entire program. She was going to call a town meeting with the new mayor and town council. Robertson was now more trouble than he was worth. He may not be the one to do the damage, but he sure could incite someone to do it.

Marcy wanted to punch that bigoted Bible reader in the mouth, even if it only made things worse. If only they had something to keep him busy with.

In her heart of hearts, Marcy knew that not all religious people were like him, and that many of them had come to her church to see how they worshiped. That was fine, and they left having a spirit-filled time in worship. More than a few went back and reported that the churches in Four Corners were just as good in preaching the Word as theirs were.

But Robertson had television and the power to reach millions more daily than they ever could. Then it hit her, along with the biggest smile she ever wore.

She ran over to her church, Four Corners Baptist. Reverend Daniels would want to hear this.

Robertson watched his troops as they made the studio ready for the day's taping. It was their special "Focus on the Family" series of shows, which he had at least three times a year. Robertson was proud of his own family, and was happy that his eldest son joined him on the show. Greg would lead the series, and he would weigh in with wise interpretation of the Bible. That the donations were always higher in these series didn't hurt either.

Greg Robertson glanced over at his father and smiled. He did like his job, and it allowed him to travel with his wife Mary Jane, who usually managed to glow with a thousand watt smiles that didn't look phony. "You ready, kids?" Robertson asked as he checked himself in the monitor.

"Oh yeah," Greg said.

"Waiting for it," replied Mary Jane.

The music came up, along with flashy graphics and a stentorian voice booming over it all. "Welcome to the Spirit Club! Today Jimmy Robertson will discuss what can be done about the town of Four Corners, plus, the emergence of gays into the mainstream, and the revelation of God's plan for it all! This and more today on the Spirit Club!"

The graphics faded and the camera flew over the audience then a cut to a floor camera as it pushed into a tight three shot of the Robertsons sitting on three chairs in a semi-circle. "Hello and welcome to the Spirit Club; as always I am Jimmy Robertson, and this my son Greg and his lovely wife whom I'm proud to call daughter, Mary Jane. We have a full show today, featuring the possible answers to the horrifying enigma that is the town of Four Corners. . . "

He was cut off by a commotion from the right of the stage. The noise was singing mixed with furious shouts of guards unable to keep the invaders out. The hymn being sung was joyous, with unabashed glee and prayerfulness. Robertson stood up in amazement. It was the people from Four Corners. It took him too long to regain his composure, but not his son. Greg Robertson stood up and faced the crowd of hymn singing invaders who knew the show was going live on its' satellite feed to the stations that would broadcast it later in various time slots.

"What do you people think you are doing?!" Greg shouted over the song.

The choir finished up and the Reverend Jacob McCandless smiled, took Greg's hand, shook it and said. "Brother, we have come to show you something. We have come to show you don't have to be afraid of us." McCandless smiled and stepped to the center of the set. "Ladies and gentlemen, I even dare call you brothers and sisters. Let me tell you what I physically am. I am a mutant. A mutant is a sudden and unexpected change in a species. Something that's unexpected." He smiled again. "I must admit, we are unexpected. Now, I don't know how you feel about that, but let me tell you something; if you keep your hand in the Lord's, you have nothing to fear. Let me repeat that. . ."

"Say it Reverend!" Someone in the choir that came with him said.

"'IF YOU KEEP YOUR HAND IN THE LORD'S, YOU HAVE NOTHING TO FEAR!" McCandless had on his full head of steam now, and even the Robertsons could see they weren't going to stop him. He opened his Bible and read from the twenty-third psalm. When he finished, he locked his eyes with the gathered in the studio audience. "You say you trust the Lord? Do you really? If you are sitting here letting a man fill you with fear of things or people who are different, YOU.... DON'T.... TRUST.... IN.... THE.... LORD!"

McCandless' lower arms went akimbo as he pointed to individual members, some of who flinched from the truth of his words. "This man talks about revival of the country, but he's forgetting about his own spirit, club!" There was nervous laughter, from the studio audience. "You have to understand, that if you have come to the Lord, there is nothing that anyone can do to your body. I want you to understand this: if you truly walk with the Lord, you have the one that will not desert you. The good Reverend Robertson must feel that God has deserted him, and he's going to do his level best to make you feel the same."

McCandless turned to the astonished, shocked Robertsons. "I'm so very sorry you are afraid of us. But we don't mean you any harm, none of us. We too, lived in fear for a long time, and that's over and no one, not me, not you, can go back. I'm going to pray for you Brother Robertson. We all will, to see if you will allow the Lord to take your fear away." He turned to the choir. "Will you take us out with 'Walk with Me Precious Lord'? I think that with all that is happening, we need it more than ever." He turned to the audience. "If you know the words, sing with us, for we need to remember that we all need to walk with the Lord when we are troubled. We need to remember that faith is the one thing that keeps our souls alive.

That Grace is what makes our lives bearable, and if we have the courage of our faith, nothing can harm us. Tell me, do you have faith? Have you received Grace?" McCandless pulled a small sharp knife, held it up, and then drew it across his palm. He held up the wound so that all could see the color of the blood. "My bleeding is nothing compared to the bleeding Christ did for me, and I am his. Are you?" He wrapped his hand in a white cloth he pulled from his robe. "Let's go." He looked at the audience for the last time. "Faith and Grace, and the courage of that," He left singing with the choir.

"We will walk by faith,
Not by sight!
For the eyes can deceive!
Unless you have faith and believe,
You're not walking with Jesus at all!
Grace, is what we have,
When we believe!
Not even the devil can deceive!
If you don't believe,
Then you cannot receive!
You're not walking with Jesus at all!"

The Robertsons were flabbergasted. Nothing was destroyed, no one was hurt and they were still alive. It took him a moment to notice, but Greg Robertson saw the people in the audience were leaving. He looked at his father and wife as they looked each other and said nothing. McCandless had proven his point, and gained new credibility by coming here.

As he exited the studio, McCandless found the choir stopped by reporters who'd been waiting since the news of their arrival had spread like wildfire and the gathered press was watching him as he joined his companions. An excited reporter ran up to him followed by others. Someone in the choir must have told them about what just happened.

Microphones were shoved in his face, and the barrage of questions began.

"Did you come here to attack the Robertsons?"

"No, we came to share what we felt was the true spirit of Christ," said McCandless.

"Do you think you've done any good?"

"I certainly hope so. I don't think we can really stop him from expressing his fears, but at the very least, we can say what we believe to be the truth."

"And what truth is that?"

"That if you have the true faith, you don't need to fear anybody, or anything. You in the media have really sensationalized our existence, and we think we had better speak up and say something in our defense before someone makes a decision we'll regret."

"Do you believe this is a start?"

"I know it's a start. I also know that no matter what, my God has a place for me, and it isn't under someone else's boot." McCandless held up his hands for silence. "The town of Four Corners' fate has been discussed by everyone else but us. Let me say that again. Our fate has been discussed by everyone else but us. This is no way for this to go on. This is no way for us to be living in fear of the world. You can destroy our bodies, but you cannot destroy our souls. You can destroy our town, but we will have been here and until the last person who was alive at this time dies, we will be remembered, and you will remember that you had to destroy us because you, not us, were scared. We will do what we can to calm the situation down. Anybody can say anything they want," McCandless had the gathered mesmerized, and he had a full head of steam up. His voice was thunderous, and he made everyone of those people listen to every word.

"Every last one of you has a part to play in this. All we're asking for is a fair hearing. And if you cannot, then what happens is partly your fault. Yes, we are different, but if you treat us as an enemy, we will be your enemy, and we will go down fighting; your choice. But I think, in this case, God may very well be on our side, but I think He will be weeping because we all will have lost our way again."

McCandless looked at the reporters. "However you see us, is how you report us. But we are not your enemy." He smiled. "God bless all of us. Good bye." He turned to the choir. "Let's go home. We got work to do."

The reporters took a while to shake off the mesmerizing sermon they'd just received, and started to call out more questions, but it was useless. The bus was loaded, and the driver, wearing a huge grin, put it in gear and drove off.

Jimmy Robertson had come out and watched the entire scene. McCandless made him look like an amateur in the worst way. His son and daughter in law also realized they were going to fall out of public favor if they handled this wrong. They couldn't stop the satellite feed, and they knew someone had recorded this. It was bad enough he'd spotted three of the mutants with cameras. The press would want to see the show they didn't want to show, and the Reverend McCandless had stirred the normally apathetic media into frenzy. McCandless was no fool. He'd come to the heart of the enemy camp and triumphed, since most of the audience was gone, and the media outside his studio had heard him and listened. They were leaving now. A cameraman pointed out Robertson to his reporter, and she approached him.

"Reverend Robertson, has this changed your mind about the people of Four Corners?" She asked. "That was a very stirring sermon he just delivered. Do you have an answer to that?"

Robertson was still lost in his own little world, and then he came back. "Excuse me, could you repeat the question?"

The reporter did so, and Robertson said: "I can't really answer you about that right now, I'll issue a statement later."

"Forgive me Reverend, but could it be that you really don't have an answer to what he just said, and whatever he said in your studio? You realize of course, if you edit the footage to make them look bad, they will still have the footage they shot, and you will look desperate to prove this man is the anti-Christ. I can get the footage you were sending to your member stations."

Robertson's face tightened into a more a grimace than a smile. "I'm sure you will."

Once inside the studio, Jimmy Robertson and family sat in the bleachers facing the set. The place was empty, except for the crew. The feed had stopped after one of the cameramen went out and got footage of McCandless preaching to the reporters, and the damage was done. He had to figure out something, but he didn't know what. That mutant preacher had made him feel like a coward, and his first foray into Four Corners hadn't been a success. "Why don't you go on home? Call Jack and see if he can sub for me while I think this thing over...."

"Dad, maybe there's a way to make peace with these people? If you keep attacking, you can lose even more credibility." Greg told him. "I never thought it was a good idea to go after them in the first place, trying to make bogey men of them. . . ."

"Then why didn't you say anything?" His father asked, not a little annoyed.

Greg didn't flinch. "Because, you're too stubborn when you get something in your head and nobody can talk you out of it. That man just came in here and told the world they will fight back. Everything that's happened in the last few weeks proves him right. When the mayor took that bullet for the President that made him a hero you can't erase. They've done a lot of good works. . ."

"Not good works, remember?" answered his father.

Greg's frustration was in his voice. ". . . . Even going to Vietnam; trying to help clean up the environment is another. Dad, they even figured out what happened to them and took that and stated helping people whose children have birth defects. Right now, no matter how much you dress it up, you, we, are coming off like a bunch of cowardly bigots." He stood up. "Dad, I think we're gonna lose, and big." Greg took Mary Jane's hand and left his father alone in the studio. The crew heard what Greg said and were leaving at the same time.

Jimmy Robertson never felt so alone in all his life.

McCandless sat in his office at the church, smiling. The reporters had gotten the footage they'd shot, and Robertson had very few options to play. But Robertson wasn't a fool that was sure. McCandless knew what was up, and surely, the good Reverend would figure out a way to come out on top. There was still work to do. If he got together with his fellow preachers in town and held a town wide revival and invited pastors, their choirs and their congregations from the surrounding towns, which might just be too much for Robertson to fight.

No saints, all sinners, and perhaps the biggest chance to make people think about everything that was surrounding the town.

It was worth a chance.

It would also be the biggest roll of the dice.

McCandless picked up the phone and punched the first number.

It took two days to gather all the choirs of the churches in Four Corners. The pastors of the churches were going to do the biggest marathon revival the parts had ever seen. More than that, it was an opportunity to worship with the other churches outside of the community.

No matter what happened, this would go down as one of the biggest revivals ever. They had even invited nationally known ministers to preach. For those so inclined, it would be wonderful. For the cynics, it was the opportunity they could not pass up. For the even more cynical, it was all show.

So be it, said McCandless. As far as he was concerned, don't come, but you were going to miss a joy filled time in the Lord.

It happened over three days.

Three days of pure preaching, singing and prayer. The media who covered it were amazed the town could pull it off.

And everyone commented how more than a few televangelists were there, with the exception of Jimmy Robertson.

For his part, Robertson made no mention of the revival himself, letting his son Greg go there and bring back reports, nodding his head in approval while swallowing his pride. As long as his fellow televangelists went there, anything he might say would be construed as sour grapes on his part.

But he would be back in their lives as soon as the hype died down, he hoped. He would be smarter about it, he hoped.

20. GAMES BEST NOT PLAYED

The trial of the would-be presidential assassin was moved to Atlanta.

This surprised no one in Four Corners. The feeling that the man could not get a fair trial in town was solid outside town. The town was sure he wouldn't make it to the courthouse.

The federal marshals made sure that he was transported at night when the town was asleep.

Imagine their surprise when the entire town showed up along the route holding candles. Some burned the murderer of Mike Conners in effigy, but there was no noise from them, their eyes burning a hole into the armored car that transported him. He scrunched down, the bravado that had sustained him failing him.

Keith Randolph Marston was thirty-three years old. When he'd heard of the town of Four Corners, he liked what Peter Devires, Junior tried to do. When he heard the president was to go there, he thought the man was insane and had to be stopped. He was going to embrace these freaks. He had to do something, and teach others not to do the same thing.

He was right, wasn't he?

He would be all right once he was out of the town. Then he saw the townspeople lined along the route, holding those candles, staring at him.

It was more than unnerving, it was horrifying. Even the federal judge who got the case knew that he got off on an insanity plea, Marston would not see the next day.

In Atlanta, the trial began when the prosecutor faced the jury and showed what he would try to prove that he'd felt he had to stop these people who had only tried to cope with what happened to them. That they lost their mayor by assassination only seemed to prove their point.

The defense was just as sure they could prove that Marston was provoked by listening to people like Jimmy Robertson railing against these people and filling them with fear of how they looked, that he wasn't at fault and suffered temporary insanity because of these and other speeches in the same mold.

The trail was sensational. Tommy Moore from WAFC television had commentary every night on every move the prosecution and the defense made. There wasn't much he or any one from the town could really do since it was out of their hands. But the media in Four Corners had interviews with the citizens that left no doubt where the town stood. More than a few in the town wanted to pull Marston out of jail and hang him.

The trial was televised. There were several attempts by the defense to delay or even get the trial moved to another state on the grounds that no impartial jury could be found. The judge denied the motion since even if they moved the trial; opinions about Four Corners were everywhere.

The absolute bombshell was dropped when Jimmy Robertson was called as a prosecution witness. When reached for comment, Robertson didn't. After some three weeks, Robertson was at the state courthouse in Atlanta; as he entered, there were signs, both supportive and against him.

The district attorney, William Smith, fixed Robertson with a steel gaze. "Reverend Robertson, when you first heard of the town of Four Corners, what was your first reaction?"

Robertson knew this was it, he was going to be held responsible for this man. Very well, he would try to fight it. "My first reaction was shock, then horror."

"Why?" asked Smith.

"I felt that they were not in God's plan for this world."

"I may assume that you found evidence in the Bible?"

"Objection, your honor; prosecution is leading the witness." Thornton Jackson said. "Many people would feel the Bible is specific about what was said about how man was supposed to look."

"Your honor, what council is forgetting that many people use the Bible to justify their actions? While it may seem inappropriate, the Reverend is well known for his interpretation of the Bible, and how it should be applied in one's life."

Judge Raymond Halpern knew he would be putting religious beliefs on trial if he gave to the prosecution. He mulled it over for a moment, then said: "objection overruled. In this case, it may be pertinent. Proceed."

Robertson swallowed hard. Now he was on trial. He looked at the D.A. and said: "It say in the Bible that man was created in God's image. It does not say that God has four arms and double pupil eyes."

"But many people would say that African Americans weren't in God's plans either; nor the Native Americans, or the Chinese, or the Japanese, even South Sea Islanders. You know what kinds of things were done to people in the Middle East during the crusades. Are you that sure about the people of Four Corners?" said Smith.

Robertson looked at Smith. "I only know that my God did not mean for people to be born like that."

"So, do you believe that anything and everything done to that town is justified?"

"Objection, your Honor!" Jackson said. "Prosecution is leading the witness."

"Overruled; answer the question." Halpern said.

"I believe we have a right to protect ourselves from any miscegenation with these people. I believe they should be sterilized to prevent them from having any more children." Robertson knew he was dead with a lot of people, and that he would be seen as persecuting people who'd done nothing to him. So be it. He would make clear what he thought. "They are not natural! They are a mistake and should be stopped from recreating themselves through their children. . . ." He stopped seeing the horrified look on more than a few faces. There were a few that agreed with him, of course. But the majority of faces wore looks of horror, knowing that the town would arm themselves to the teeth. He continued. "I cannot help but feel sorry for those that think they will not try to procreate with normal human beings. It will happen, and it may happen to one of your sons or daughters. I feel sorry for those of you who would welcome them into normal society. We will be damned because of you. I salute the young man who tried to prevent the mistake the president made of embracing these freaks." He fell silent.

Smith stared at Robertson for a long time. "No more questions, Your Honor."

"No questions, Your Honor." Jackson said. The look on his face said it all.

Marston couldn't even make half a coherent statement in his own defense. The jury, after hearing what Robertson said, pretty much figured that Marston figured he would get off if he used Robertson as his defense. It didn't work. He got life.

The people of Four Corners cheered and partied, but they soon calmed down.

Life would go on, but they didn't take anything for granted.

Four Corners cleaned up the town, held its' funerals, and tried to start over. More people who had been affected by the river water further downstream moved into town. The place was doing all it could to get back to whatever "normal" was. They took in the newcomers with as open a heart as they could manage, and did everything they could to make them feel welcome. The healing would take time.

Sam Warner stood up to speak, knowing this was the most important speech he would give. He stood in front of his fellows in the Congress. His gaze was steady and firm.

"Thank you, Mister Speaker. I would like to remind my friend here in Congress that our job is not to succumb to the fear mongering and panic that some people would have us make our own."

"The people of Four Corners are still citizens of this country, and they deserve a chance to live their lives like any American. I say they have already proven their worth. I say they have done more for this country than we can ever thank them for. By making the effort to learn, on their own, they have shown the kind of initiative that we say we value, the kind of courage that make for great citizens."

"We cannot allow for the sort of fear that leads to bad lawmaking. We cannot show the world that fear guides our system of government, that the majority fear of a minority, no matter how unusual they are in their appearance, customs or language, will force our hand. Anything else would be genocide. I want the members of congress who believe that to force these people, the people of Four Corners to do something they already do, that is, isolate them by choice. If they should desire to leave their town, they should be able to while taking the common sense precautions that anyone else would take. I say that we have nothing to fear unless we provoke them, like anyone else. We must not succumb to bigotry, and demand that they become prisoners in their own homes by law. Thank you."

Senator James Davis came to the podium. "Thank you Mister Speaker. I would like to point out that our young colleague is from Four Corners. This should not be seen as a blot against him, but should be seen as being too close to the situation. I can understand his unwillingness to see his town isolated. But one can only wonder why he and his wife had not had children if the town were so harmless. . ."

"Mr. SPEAKER, I MUST OBJECT!" Warner shouted with fury from his seat, standing.

"I have the floor, Senator!" Davis said. "I HAVE THE FLOOR!" Davis turned to the speaker, then back to Warner. "I must ask that the senator allow me to finish!"

The speaker brought his gavel down several times as the room erupted in chaos. "Senator Davis has the floor. Continue, Senator."

"Thank you, Mr. Speaker." Davis said. "As I was saying, if the town was so harmless, why haven't Senator Warner and his wife had children? There must be a reason, and it may be in the town itself. I do understand about their very legitimate fears. But they must also understand that we must be sure that whatever has so deformed them is under control. I urge that we assure the American people that they will be safe." He paused for dramatic effect, and then continued. "If we don't make sure, absolutely sure, that what happened does not happen again, we could see the end of normal human beings in this country."

This brought a huge chorus of boos and catcalls and Sam Warner to the other podium. He waited there, fuming.

Davis turned to Warner and said; "I realize, Senator that you feel the instinctive urge to protect your family and friends, but you must realize that we have to make sure we are protected. I don't want to see that town become a concentration camp any more than you do. You cannot begrudge us the need to make sure that our future is secure. Our children are our future, Senator, and I will not risk that."

Warner wore the deepest fury on his face. "I cannot tell you how much that sort of talk only precedes the isolation and disenfranchising of people. If the speaker will allow it, I can read you the accomplishments of this town, and how they've, we've done to make sure it that what caused our mutations do not happen to others. And as for my wife and I not having a child yet, while that is none of your business, I will tell that we are working on it. I suppose the senator would like to watch?" This brought a chorus of laughter. "The facts are these. . ." Warner proceeded to tell Four Corners story and the toll it took and challenge it gave to a people who were forced to look to themselves for the answers, all the time knowing that it would go into the Congressional Record, and at the same time not caring, his voice strong and clear, he made sure that everything they learned became public knowledge. They hadn't been experts when they started, but now, they knew maybe more than some of the "experts" in those fields. The story had the desired effect. He could see how the members sat with their eyes riveted to him. "My fellow members of Congress, the facts are simple; yes my brother and sister are four armed. Yes, the town has a majority of multiple armed people, and more are being born right now, I'm sure. It may be that my wife and I will have a multiple limbed child. But none of this is reason to panic. And no, I don't think anyone will have those limbs hacked off since they are part and parcel of who and what they are. I have no doubt that if there was an unenforceable law prohibiting multiple limbs passed, you would see a blood bath in this country the likes you've never seen. I caution the good Senator Davis; do not run against my hometown. Because if something does happen to outlaw the people of Four Corners, I can promise you this--it will not be pretty, and whatever fears you have now will only be multiplied. No one likes to be bullied, Senator, and you will find the people of Four Corners more than ready to take you and any other who thinks they can push them around on. You throw down the gauntlet, Senator; you better get ready to fight."

Davis knew he'd blown it, big. "I would like to clarify my remarks. Perhaps I did not make myself clear. I did not say we should try and outlaw or isolate the town. All I said was that we should be able to make sure that such an occurrence does not happen again. I did not say, nor do I mean that we make the people or the town illegal. All I said is that we need to test the river water in the southern section of this country to make sure that those who are born in the future are healthy as possible. It would be unwise to try and outlaw something like multiple limbs, since said limbs are an accident of nature, and not a deliberate action on the towns' part. I apologize to the Senator Warner and the people of Four Corners for any remarks that may have been misconstrued."

He sat down, and the senator next to him said: "Nice recovery. He was ready to kill you."

"Tell me about it." Davis said. "There's no way we could have made them outlaws, anyway. My grandson thinks they're cool."

21. RESOLUTION ONE

Cody Macabee was almost done with the examinations. He was grateful he could make sure that there was as thorough a job as possible. He was sick of the hospital and almost as sick of the people. He was tired of the poking and prodding, the constant questions, most of which were really simple and annoying at best.

In any case, Cody knew his father had given his interview, he'd given his, and the town would survive, even with the loss of Mike Conners. He'd been safe in the hospital and followed the events in town on television like everyone, and they watched him for his reactions, even monitoring his heart.

Cody was allowed visitors, and they were examined just as he was, even his Cousin Frank's little boy, Jeffrey rightly howled as the strangers did unto him as they did unto his father. Even his Aunt Mercer came for a visit, and found her DNA being gathered just so they could compare her and Cody.

But it was almost over, and even Doctor Theresa St. Thomas was glad. It meant now all she had to do was make sense of it all. "You realize I'm going with a team to Four Corners, don't you?"

"It figures." Cody said as he packed his things. "You, the EPA and Lord only know who else will be moving in there, and that makes me kind of angry. I like that we stayed a small town. I guess that's over. I'm going to miss it."

"You make it sound like there's been a death in the family." St. Thomas said, not a little annoyed. "You'll just have to get used to us having to study you."

"That's BS and you know it." Cody returned. "Let's face it, you just want to keep an eye on us, and see how we handle what's coming." He looked away. "I would have to miss the revival. . ."

"I didn't know you were religious." St. Thomas said, "You Baptist?"

"Yeah, You?" asked Cody.

"Methodist," She replied.

"Methodist to your madness then," He shot back.

St. Thomas groaned. "That joke is older than dirt."

"Heh!" snorted Cody. "It's been real." He picked up his bags, and moved to the door. "Look, I know from here on out, everything has changed. I guess, I just want us to be as safe as possible, and that is not gonna happen. I'm scared, Theresa, and I don't think I'm not gonna be the same again. For me, there's just too much at stake. I blame myself for what's happened, and what is gonna happen. Up until my accident, my people were safe. They never will be again." He left her in his room.

St. Thomas ran after him and grabbed his lower right arm. "You listen to me, damn it! It had to happen! You guys were gonna be found out sooner or later. It just happened sooner. It might have happened when you were on a cleanup job, or like it happened to you. That's how the dice roll sometimes. This time, snake eyes; next time, who knows?"

Cody gave her a weak smile. "Yeah, well, who knows, right?" He looked down the hallway. There were reporters at the other end. "Snake eyes, again."

He took two steps. "I understand Dane Taylor of the DUP is moving to new offices down there. Is Doctor Harris coming with you?"

"No, he's got to make sense of those findings while we take a good hard look at the town. He'll join us later." St. Thomas replied. "I've got news for you; he really likes you and wishes you'd forgive him that first day. He didn't know any more than we did." They came to the desk so Cody could be released. "But I have to tell you that he wants to go down there as soon as possible. He's talking about getting a corpse to examine since you're so uncooperative."

"Ehhuch, what a sicko! There are probably a couple of cadavers, but they go to the medical school. We'll see." Cody said as he signed out. The other doctors joined them, and it occurred to one of them they'd just given the media a great photo opportunity. They talked for a few minutes, all of them wishing Cody a good trip home.

His good-byes finished, Cody sighed and went to the reporters who gave him walking space, although matching his pace.

"Cody, do you think the town will be alright after the death of the mayor?"

Cody replied: "I know I'll miss him, like everyone will and does, but I think the town will survive."

"Cody, do you think the government will do anything to isolate the town, and perhaps sterilize the citizens?"

"I certainly hope not," said Cody, making his way to the front door.

"Do you believe that Four Corners will be a major military base as it's been speculated?"

"That's a new one to me. I don't think so." Cody saw there was a Ford Crown Victoria waiting for him, with his father standing at the rear door. As he made his way to the car, his father opened the trunk, and helped his son toss his bags in.

"Monsieur Le Cody! Do you believe that your people will get fair treatment from now on?"

"I'm praying about that!" Cody said as his father ducked in the car and he followed. Eric Pierpont drove off.

"Glad to get you out of the circus, Cody." Eric said.

"Thank you. I'm tired of questions. I'm sick of talking." Cody said as he settled into his seat.

Bodine smiled. "I don't think I blame you. Those reporters can talk your ears off!"

Cody laughed. "Tell me about it! I should tell you, the doctors that examined me, plus Dane Taylor, the guy from the Department of Unusual Phenomena, will be coming to town, permanently."

"Well thank you Santa Claus!" Eric said with disgust. "That explains the government types that rented that building on Maple and Richmond."

The old Crowley and Haber store?" asked Cody.

"Yeah; you know Belinda's been trying to unload it for years. I understand they hired Hutchinson's company to do the remodeling," Said Eric.

"I bet Mike's happy." Bodine said.

"He's glad about the work; he's just not crazy about the client." They all laughed, and then Eric sobered. "Listen, Cody."

"Yeah...?"

"Don't blame yourself, man. It had to happen. You know, I consider us lucky that you were the one it happened to."

"Oh? Why?"

"Cause your daddy didn't raise no dummy. You did good. You made us look good."

"You really think so?"

"Boy," Bodine said with pride, "you showed them we weren't monsters, but people. No matter what happens from here on out, you were the first they met. You handled them with style. You did good."

Cody felt warm inside. His fears were lifting about any betrayal on his part. They knew it was an accident. "Thank you."

"Just thought you needed to know, son." Bodine said quietly. "Sometimes a man makes history; sometimes he gets caught up in it. You got caught up in it. The fact remains, we're known now, and wishin' ain't gonna change it."

"Tell me about it," Said Eric. "The government wants all our research in DNA, including the work on the genome we've done. They say they want to compare it to what they've got. I don't like the sound of it."

"You and everybody else," Bodine said grimly. "Town council's gonna meet to see what we're gonna say; most likely to be yes, just to keep them from coming in and taking work in progress from us. Things change, boys. That's the only thing constant in life."

They drove in silence for a while, with only a country station softly playing something by Dolly Parton. The three joined in as the song ended, then joined again when Hank Williams, Junior started.

The council room was packed that morning, with Cody and Bodine getting there early to get a seat.

The new mayor, Frank Swearlow, was waiting for Cody, Bodine and Eric as they drove up, watched as the car pulled up to the City Hall steps and they got out. The crowd roared for its returning brother and Cody waved to them and smiled. Swearlow shook his hand. "You did well, Cody."

Jake Carrow stepped to the four men with a microphone. "Cody, it's good to have you back home. How are you feeling now?"

"It's good to be home, Jake. I know most of you don't blame me for what happened, but I still feel responsible that we were finally found out after all these years, and I am sorry. I just hope we can get to some semblance of sanity, now."

"Well, I think I can say that it wasn't your fault for the accident. I think you handled everything with as much care as possible, and I don't blame you at all." Jake said. The crowd roared in agreement. "Welcome home Cody." He shook his hand.

"Thanks." Cody replied.

Frank Swearlow leaned in the microphone and said: "Cody, don't worry about it. We've survived this long without the government here in Four Corners and we'll survive with the government here in Four Corner. Your friends and neighbors are ready for whatever happens."

"That's good to know." Cody said, trying to put on as good a face as he could. But the new Mayor wasn't saying what he and everyone in town knew---everything had changed, and no matter how you dressed it up, they were in new, uncharted waters.

Jimmy Robertson watched the giant screen television showing Cody's homecoming. The four-armed man was being given a hero's welcome, and it galled him. The freaks were going on with their lives after this little demonstration.

Robertson thought back to that choir coming to his studio and facing him down on his own turf. The worse thing was that someone from CNN had been watching and recorded the invasion. McCandless had preached beautifully, he thought ruefully, beautifully enough to make his own son quit his father's ministry and start his own. It was almost too much.

Had he lost his faith? Lost his way?

He hoped not.

It was almost too much to ask that he reconsider his stand on the town and people.

No scratch that.

It was too much to ask him to reconsider.

Every bone in his body was screaming that he was right. But there was no way to prove it.

The resolution had to come.

It had to.

Peter Devires, Junior had found refuge in a small town in the Oklahoma panhandle. He dyed his hair dark and grew a beard that he kept dyed too.

He also watched Cody's homecoming on a small black and white television while drinking a flat Budweiser from last night. His cousin let him stay in the trailer behind the house that served as a guesthouse. His cousin's wife objected loud and long about him staying there since the only time he showed up was when he was on the run from some kind of trouble.

His cousin let him stay on the condition he did nothing to draw attention to himself.

Devires knew he was in trouble if his cousin's wife decided to blow the whistle on him.

So he would be quiet. But those freaks that got him on the run would get theirs, he'd see to that.

The resolution had to come.

It had to.

Frank Swearlow sat on his front porch puffing away on his pipe as his wife joined him. She didn't mind the pipe as long as it wasn't in the house. He looked over at Jess as she worked on pieces for a quilt. She sat down in the swing and began to gently rock back and forth as she cut the pieces out of fresh cloth.

"It's good to have Cody back. . ." she said absently.

"It is. . . "

"I can't help but think about all those people who died."

"You don't blame him, do you?" He asked, relighting his pipe.

"No, not really," She said as she dropped a piece into her basket. "It's just. . . ."

"What?" Frank asked looking at her.

"I think that with everything that's gone on, maybe we shouldn't have raised such a fuss over him coming home." Jess said. "It made him look like we wasn't expecting him to come back."

"Did you expect him to come back?" Frank asked, fixing his gaze on her.

"No I didn't." Jess said, "I won't tell that lie. Didn't anybody expect him to come back...."

"Then we were right to celebrate him coming back alive. After that deal in the sixties with the Army, not too many of us did come back, remember?" Frank said firmly, relighting his pipe again. "Even I lost my right eye. It only takes one to see some of us will not be staying alive after this. Baby, don't you see? People are scared of us, and they won't stop being scared. We're not the enemy, but we're not their friends, either."

"Either way, I don't want to live in fear," Jess said sadly, "there's got to be a resolution. There's just got to be."

22. RESOLUTION TWO

The senior senator sat in the in the governor's office in Atlanta. Both men wore grim faces as they watched Cody Macabee's homecoming.

"Damn. . ." the governor said, drumming his fingers on the arm of his big leather chair. "Frankly, I don't mind them being here in the state, but I do mind they might be targets for every loony in the country. Now, I've got to tell you, they've generate a hell of a lot of taxes, and I don't want to lose that. . ."

"Naturally. . ." said the senator.

". . . but we also have to reassure the people of this state that they were not our idea!" The governor said firmly. "I got more letters about the town of Four Corners than anything else in the last three months." He rubbed his temples. "I got to tell you, I expect that town to get mighty shaken up in the next year. I expect it to be a donnybrook over how that place continues from here on out. Damn! We're living a science fiction film!"

"And you can't bring out the army, because they are the victims." The senator laughed. "You know, my grandson thinks they're cool. Toy companies are making offers; Hollywood wants to make a movie of them." Both men chuckled heartily. "Know what I say?"

"What?"

"Do nothing."

"What..?..!"

"Do nothing."

"Why the hell do you say that..?..!"

"Because, any town that has managed to get along without us and doesn't need us trying to tell them what to do," He leaned back in the chair. "One, don't make it sound like you're gonna come to their rescue, they don't need you, or us. Two, let's not be afraid of them. Remember, they're more scared of us, than we are of them. That's what that whole homecoming thing was about. I'm going to advise the president to do the same."

"What if he doesn't agree?"

"He'll have to. Right now there's a lot of sympathy for them out there and even if it winds down. . ."

"Which it will. . ."

"They will fight you tooth, fang and nail. You don't need enemies who can do unto us what was accidentally done to them."

"Keeping quiet's not gonna be easy."

"Neither fighting an unnecessary enemy; right now, they're quiet, good taxpaying citizens. Who can do things we don't know about? To hell with sterilizing them, to hell with a concentration camp, just let them be who they are, and they will find their new level."

The governor stared at the senator. It was good, common sense advice. "Fine, I guess the only thing I can do is make a tour that goes through the town, that way it won't look like I'm just making a good on a photo opportunity."

"Makes a damn good one though...."

The president sat in the conference room with his entire cabinet. They'd discussed the town for hours, after having discussed it for days in smaller groups. The town represented to the president a troubling problem. How do you acknowledge them and not look like you're favoring them. He'd made two trips there already, one ending with the death of their mayor. The funeral was bad enough with that one man pointing at him and screaming it was his fault that Conners died. That the man was lead away wasn't the point.

Many in the town when questioned blamed him for setting the mayor up as part of a plan by the government to take over. It was denied, of course, but the town's fear that there would be some kind of takeover was hard to calm.

"Who's the new mayor again?" asked the president.

"Frank Swearlow, sir." One aide said. "He was the deputy mayor, sworn in to office the next day to keep a lid on the town."

"He did a good job." The president said. "What I want to know is, do we approach him or not?"

"I think we should at the least acknowledge he's there. I don't know if we should invite him to the White House yet."

"Tell you this; we should make sure that we let him know that we have them in mind, even if we never say anything to them again." A second aide said.

"To be frank, Mr. President, I don't think we're even on their minds." A third aide spoke. "My feeling is they will do what they can to get back to what passes for normal. After that, who knows?"

The silence dropped like a weight, allowing each person in the room to think about these people and this town. Then the president spoke.

"Do we know if there are any other places like this in the country?"

His aides looked at each other. They knew some of the towns downstream had mutants, but other parts of the country?

It scared them.

It was possible.

It was time they found out.

"I want a survey done on all major industrial areas, preferably on a local level. It might be voluntary, with help from the EPA. First we have aliens, and now mutants. What the hell is going on here?" The president rubbed his temples and sighed. "I've got a feeling this is just the start. I don't think normal people will be in any real danger, but we should know the extent of mutations in this country, their shape and form, and whether or not they can reproduce. Four Corners' mutations are fairly benign, but any other may be less so, and we should be ready for what may come up. Four Corners stays isolated by choice for the most part, and only really comes out to do business. That's no problem, and they are ready, for the most part to take on those who say they should never live. I say, as long as they're on their best behavior, fine. They know how it would go if they break the law." He looked at his team. "This has importance, people, because we may have done it to ourselves. I want to know just how bad." He saw heads nodding in agreement. "Let's do it."

Cody Macabee sat in his booth at the diner. Marcy had just set his plate before him when Joyce Madisen came in. She pointed to the seat opposite him and asked: "is this seat taken?" Cody shook his head no and she sat down.

They sat in silence except for the order Marcy took for a chef's salad with the dressing on the side, and an ice tea with lemon and Sweet 'N' Low. Cody dug into his double chicken fried steak. Her order came and she began. They ate in silence with Joyce taking a glance or two at her silent dining partner.

They finished, and the table was cleared and both had a pound cake sundae supreme with whipped cream and nuts. Joyce had hers with the pitcher of fudge.

"You're having that with the pitcher of fudge after you had tea with Sweet 'N' Low?!" Cody was incredulous.

"Don't laugh, my sister's worse," said Joyce, "I do have one question for you. . ."

"Shoot."

"Did you drive me to New York the first time I came through here?"

Cody smiled. "No."

"Damn. . ." Joyce said, disappointed. "Would have made some nice symmetry . . ."

"Tell me about it." Cody said as he drew his spoon through ice cream and cake. "By the way, I liked your pieces on the town. They were pretty tough, but fair."

"That's me, trying to do it right. I don't like rushing to judgment. I figure you guys had been through enough already." She poured more of the fudge over what was left.

Cody was bemused. "Do you do this every time you wrap a story?"

"No, just for the big ones, or when I'm really stressed but, let me tell you something; People are gonna come here, no matter what. I don't want to say it, but you'd better be ready to try and control the way the freak show goes, 'cause it will go."

Cody gave a wry smile. "Tell me something I don't know."

"No, I mean it. You guys have been in the closet, so to speak, for a long time, now you're out. Make sure you control how you're perceived. Lord knows, they'll eat you alive." Joyce said before she popped the next spoonful in her mouth. "I've got one suggestion. . ."

"What's that?"

"Let me help with the town's story. At the very least, it will be accurate, and the town will have it down in black and white. Might even be a best seller." Joyce smiled.

"Why tell me, and not the mayor?"

"I need someone who's been through the ringer, and can break it down so people can understand it. Interested?"

Cody thought it over. "My answer will probably be yes, but let me sleep on it."

"I can deal with that." Joyce said. Marcy came to their table with the bill. Joyce grabbed both and said: "My treat."

She got up, handed her Visa over after adding a tip to the total.

Cody stood up and faced her. "You realize I most likely know the people who got this town going. You need them, right?"

"Yeah, so does the town. This book could let off a lot of steam, Cody."

"And the miniseries, the Saturday morning cartoon, the action figures. . . "

"You're a cynic."

"Naw, just greedy; it's my, and the town's turn to make a load of money off of us." Cody said. "God bless the capitalist system."

"I was right, you are a cynic." Joyce said.

"Is that so wrong?" Cody asked. "So far I heard of at least three movies for television, a miniseries and a feature, and none of the producers talked to us. Screw it, and let us make the most money possible. It's our town, and we should have the right to tell our story."

"Sounds like you've thought about it." Joyce said as they left the diner. "You ready to write?"

Cody looked at her, and then shrugged. "I guess I am." He looked up, and even with the light from the rapidly receding diner, could see the stars. He felt like he was about to fall into the biggest, looniest trip of his life, like all that had happened was just a prelude. He saw a family of townspeople go into the restaurant, and the little boy waved at him. He waved back, as did Joyce. Two more families followed in rapid secession, and their children told him what he had to do.

"See you when the library opens?" He asked Joyce.

The next afternoon, the reporters sat at Mama Dozier's house. There were two tape recorders and a stack of blank numbered tapes along with video cameras. They'd been there most of the day, and Mama Dozier showed no signs of tiring.

"You know, children, if I knew then, what I know now..."

ABOUT THE AUTHOR

Born in Hattiesburg, Mississippi in 1958 (a year he swears was a very good one!), Kenneth Strickland grew up in California and with his family in their Chevy drove through the Watts riots and people did what he called 'Olympic shopping' while the stores burned. Like many young ones he watched Star Trek and other Science Fiction television, loves cartoons, auto racing and the Dodgers. He is an enthusiastic writer and graphic designer, and animator and loves a good view of the ocean.

www.ingramcontent.com/pod-product-compliance
Lightning Source LLC
Chambersburg PA
CBHW071713140626
46557CB00011B/85

* 9 7 8 0 9 6 2 7 8 3 5 7 9 *